# 編者的話

這本書原先只給「劉毅英文家教班」上課同學使用，孩子們都覺得這本書是無價之寶，應該把這個方法告訴大家，讓更多人受益。

背了「一口氣英語」系列的讀者，對「一口氣英語」都愛不釋手，愈背愈想背。很多人都自己在家開班授課，將這種方法傳了出去。「一口氣英語」系列，是教你完全採取主動，把想說的話背到滾瓜爛熟，要用的時候可以脫口而出。和外國人淺談，用「一口氣英語」；和外國人深談，則用「一口氣英語演講」。

但是，也有些讀者問我們，如果外國人採取主動，我們反應不過來，該怎麼辦呢？於是我們研發了「問一答三英語」，書中的每一句回答都優美得體，例如：外國人跟你說 "Good-bye." 的時候，你就可以立刻回答三句：

> Take care. （要保重。）
> Catch you later. （以後見。）
> See you again. （再見。）

書中所有的解釋，和「一口氣英語」一樣，詳詳細細，哪些問題常問，都有按照使用頻率排列，回答也可有其他不同的選擇。

英語口說測驗是未來考試的趨勢。本書附有 CD，錄音方式完全比照「多益測驗」新增加的口試型式。Track 1～10 是給你練習用的，當外國老師說："Question One. May I ask your name?" 的時候，會停適當的時間，讓你試著回答；你回答後，外國老師會說："Please repeat after me." 然後你就跟著唸："My name is Pat Smith. Everyone calls me Pat. You can call me Pat."。

　　Track 11 和 Track 12 是兩個總測驗，Track 11 是按照次序，從 Question 1 到 Question 100，給你訓練。Track 12，外國老師會不按照次序，問你整本書的 100 個問題，每一個問題都沒有唸題號（如 Question 1、Question 2 等），讓你有真實被外國人問的感覺。每個問題後空三句正常回答的時間，看你會不會回答。你要練到自己聽到每個問題，都能立即回答三句，此時，你面對外國人，就天不怕、地不怕了！

　　這種口說英語的訓練方式，你只要多聽，跟著 CD 回答、跟著 CD 唸，就可以背下來。以後聽到外國人說的話，就自然而然會有直覺的反應，他們一定會稱讚你的英語能力。

　　本書雖經審慎編校，疏漏之處恐所難免，誠盼各界先進不吝指正。

劉　毅

---

**Question 1**

# *May I ask your name?*

（未回答前，勿翻下一頁）

---

這句話的意思是「請問你的名字是什麼？」這是比較客氣的説法。要是大人問小孩的話，只説：What's your name?（你叫什麼名字？）

下面都是美國人常説的話，我們按照使用頻率排列：

① What's your name?【第一常用】
　（你叫什麼名字？）
② *May I ask your name?*【第二常用】
③ Please tell me your name.【第三常用】
　（請告訴我你的名字。）

④ Can you tell me your name?
　（你能告訴我你的名字嗎？）
⑤ Could you tell me your name?
　（你能告訴我你的名字嗎？）

⑥ What do people call you?
　（大家都怎麼叫你？）
⑦ What name do you go by?
　（你叫什麼名字？）【*go by* 被叫作】
⑧ I'd like to know your name.
　（我想知道你的名字。）

## Answers 1

### *My name is Pat Smith.*
### *Everyone calls me Pat.*
### *You can call me Pat.*

□ 答對　□ 答錯

* Pat〔pæt〕*n.* 派特　　Smith〔smɪθ〕*n.* 史密斯

這三句話的意思是:「我的名字是派特・史密斯。大家都叫我派特。你可以叫我派特。」

*You can call me Pat.* 也可說成:Just call me Pat. ( 叫我派特就好了。) 說完三句以後,你還可以接著再說:

My first name is Pat. ( 我的名字是派特。)
My last name is Smith. ( 我姓史密斯。)
That's my family name. ( 那是我的姓。)
【*first name* 名字　*last name* 姓 ( = *family name* )】

My nickname is Pat. ( 我的暱稱是派特。)
My formal name is Patrick.
( 我正式的名字是派翠克。)
All my friends call me Pat.
( 我所有朋友都叫我派特。)

nickname〔'nɪk͵nem〕*n.* 綽號;暱稱
formal〔'fɔrml̩〕*adj.* 正式的

---

Question 2

# *How old are you?*

（未回答前，勿翻下一頁）

---

這句話的意思是「你幾歲？」也可加長爲：How old are you now?（你現在幾歲？）也可客氣地說：Please tell me how old you are.（請告訴我你現在幾歲。）

下面都是美國人常說的話：

*How old are you?*【第一常用】

What's your age?（你年紀多大？）【第四常用】

What age are you?（你幾歲？）【第五常用】

When were you born?（你何時出生？）【第二常用】

In what year were you born?【第六常用】

（你出生於哪一年？）

What's your date of birth?【第三常用】

（你的出生日期是哪一天？）

【date〔det〕*n.* 日期　　birth〔bɝθ〕*n.* 出生】

What's your birth date?【第七常用】

（你的生日是哪一天？）

How many years old are you?（你幾歲？）【第八常用】

What's your current age?【第九常用】

（你現在是幾歲？）【current〔ˈkɝənt〕*adj.* 現在的】

## Answers 2

*I'm fifteen.*
*I'm fifteen years old.*
*I was born fifteen years ago.*

□ 答對　□ 答錯

　　這三句話的意思是：「我十五。我十五歲。我出生於十五年前。」

　　*I'm fifteen.* 也可簡化爲：Fifteen.（十五歲。）*I'm fifteen years old.* 也可加長爲：I'm fifteen years old this year.（我今年十五歲。）*I was born fifteen years ago.* 也可說成：I was born in 1992.（我出生於 1992 年。）

　　【比較】　下面兩句意思相同：

　　　　*I'm fifteen.*【較常用】
　　　　= I am fifteen.【常用】

　　也有美國人說：I'm fifteen this year.（我今年十五歲。）或 My age is fifteen.（我的年紀是十五歲。）如果你不想回答年齡，你就可以說：

　　　　Why do you ask?（你爲什麼要問？）
　　　　It's a secret.（這是個祕密。）
　　　　I don't want to tell you.（我不想告訴你。）
　　　　【secret〔'sikrɪt〕*n.* 祕密】

　　說這三句話時，一定要面帶微笑，否則不禮貌。

**Question 3**

# *How are you?*

（未回答前，勿翻下一頁）

　　這句話的意思是「你好嗎？」也可加長為：How are you today?（你今天好嗎？）***How are you?*** 的完成式型態是：How have you been?（你近來好嗎？）

下面都是美國人常說的話：

***How are you?***【第一常用】
How are you doing?（你好嗎？）【第二常用】
How are you feeling?（你覺得如何？）【第五常用】

How's it going?（你好嗎？）【第三常用】
How is everything?（一切都好嗎？）【第四常用】
How have you been?（你好嗎？）【第六常用】
【go〔go〕v. 進展】

What's up?（發生什麼事；你好嗎？）【第七常用】
What's new?（有什麼新鮮事；你好嗎？）【第八常用】
What's happening?【第九常用】
（發生什麼事；你好嗎？）

　　美國人打招呼用語很多，可參照「劉毅演講式英語①會話總整理①-5」。

## Answers 3

> *I'm fine.*
> *I'm doing great.*
> *Everything is great.*

□答對　□答錯

\* fine〔faɪn〕*adj.* 好的　　do〔du〕*v.* 進展
great〔gret〕*adv.* 很好地　*adj.* 極好的

這三句話的意思是:「我很好。我很好。一切都很好。」

對於 How are you? 的回答,除了上面三句外,也可以簡單地說三句:I'm fine. Thanks. And you? (我很好。謝謝。你呢?)

***I'm doing great.*** 也可說成:I'm doing good. (我很好。)【good〔gʊd〕*adv.* 好】也可加長為:I'm doing great. I couldn't be better. (我很好。我沒辦法更好了。)

也可幽默地回答:

Not so good. (不太好。)
Just so-so. (只是馬馬虎虎。)
Could be better. (可以更好。)
【so-so〔'so,so〕*adj.* 一般的;馬馬虎虎的】

**Question 4**

# *Where do you live?*

（未回答前，勿翻下一頁）

　　這句話的意思是「你住在哪裡？」可以禮貌地問：
May I ask where you live? (可以請問你住在哪裡嗎？)
或 May I ask, "Where do you live?" (可不可以請問
你：「你住在哪裡？」)

下面都是美國人常說的話：

　　*Where do you live?*【第一常用】
　　Where is your home?【第四常用】
　　（你們家在哪裡？）
　　Where is your house?【第五常用】
　　（你們家在哪裡？）

　　What's your address?【第二常用】
　　（你的地址是哪裡？）
　　What street do you live on?【第六常用】
　　（你住在哪條街？）
　　What part of town do you live in?【第三常用】
　　（你住在城裡的哪個部份？）
　　【address〔ə'drɛs〕n. 地址　　town〔taʊn〕n. 城鎮；都市】

---

**Answers 4**

*I live in Taipei.*

*I live in the city.*

*My home is not far.*

□答對　□答錯

---

\* far〔far〕*adj.* 遠的

這三句話的意思是:「我住在台北。我住在市區。我家住
得不遠。」

*I live in Taipei.* 也可說成:I live in Taipei City.
(我住在台北市。) *I live in the city.* 也可加強語氣說成:
I live right here in Taipei City. (我就住在台北市這裡。)

*My home is not far.* 可加長爲:My home is not
far away. (我家住得不遠。) 或 My home is not far
from here. (我家離這裡不遠。)

如果你家不住在台北市區,你就可以說:

I live near Taipei. (我住在台北附近。)
I live in the suburbs. (我住在郊區。)
My home is one hour away.
(我家離這裡要一小時路程。)
【suburbs〔'sʌbɝbz〕*n. pl.* 郊區】

My home is one hour away. 可以說得更清楚一點,
成爲:My home is one hour away by bus. (我家搭公
車去要一小時。)

**Question 5**

# *What are your hobbies?*

（未回答前，勿翻下一頁）

\* hobby〔'hɑbɪ〕*n.* 嗜好

　　這句話的意思是「你有什麼嗜好？」也有人說：Tell me what your hobbies are.（告訴我你有什麼嗜好。）或 Tell me some of your hobbies.（告訴我一些你的嗜好。）

【比較】***What are your hobbies?***
　　　　【由於嗜好通常不只一個，多用複數。】
　　　　*What's your hobby?*【這是書本英語，但美國人不說。】

下面是美國人常說的話：

***What are your hobbies?***【第一常用】
What are your interests?【第四常用】
（你的興趣是什麼？）
What are your pastimes?【第六常用】
（你的消遣是什麼？）
【interest〔'ɪntrɪst〕*n.* 興趣　　pastime〔'pæs,taɪm〕*n.* 消遣】

What do you like to do?（你喜歡做什麼？）【第二常用】
What activities do you enjoy?【第五常用】
（你喜歡什麼活動？）
What things do you enjoy doing?【第三常用】
（你喜歡做什麼？）
【activity〔æk'tɪvətɪ〕*n.* 活動　　enjoy〔ɪn'dʒɔɪ〕*v.* 喜歡】

**Answers 5**

*I like sports.*
*I like being outdoors.*
*I enjoy fresh air and sunshine.*

□答對　□答錯

\* sport〔sport〕*n.* 運動
outdoors〔'aut'dorz〕*adv.* 在戶外
fresh〔frɛʃ〕*adj.* 新鮮的　　air〔ɛr〕*n.* 空氣
sunshine〔'sʌn,ʃaɪn〕*n.* 陽光

　　這三句話的意思是：「我喜歡運動。我喜歡待在戶外。我喜歡新鮮的空氣和陽光。」也可以回答：

　　I like seeing movies.
　　（我喜歡看電影。）
　　I love to go hiking.
　　（我喜歡去健行。）
　　I especially like traveling abroad.
　　（我特別喜歡到國外旅行。）

　　hike〔haɪk〕*v.* 健行
　　especially〔ə'spɛʃəlɪ〕*adv.* 尤其；特別地
　　abroad〔ə'brɔd〕*adv.* 到國外

　　也可以開玩笑地說：Sleeping, watching TV, and playing computer games.（睡覺、看電視，和玩電玩遊戲。）

---

**Question 6**

# *How many are in your family?*

（未回答前，勿翻下一頁）

---

　　這句話的意思是「你家裡有幾個人？」源自：How many are there in your family?（你家裡有幾個人？）句中的 many 是名詞，How many 是問「有幾個」。可以客氣地說：Please tell me, "How many are in your family?"（請告訴我：「你家裡有幾個人？」）也可加強語氣說成：How many altogether in your family?（你家裡總共有幾個人？）【altogether〔͵ɔltə'gɛðɚ〕*adv.* 總共】

下面都是美國人常說的話：

How many in your family?（你家裡有幾個人？）【第四常用】
***How many are in your family?***【第三常用】
How many are there in your family?【第一常用】
（你家裡有幾個人？）

How many people are there in your family?
（你家裡有幾個人？）【第二常用】
How many members are there in your family?
（你家裡有幾個成員？）【第六常用】
How many members does your family have?
（你家裡有幾個成員？）【第七常用】【member〔'mɛmbɚ〕*n.* 成員】

Do you have a big family?（你們是大家庭嗎？）【第八常用】
Do you have a lot of people in your family?
（你家裡有很多人嗎？）【第九常用】
How many brothers and sisters do you have?
（你有幾個兄弟姐妹？）【第五常用】

*There are four.*
*We have four people.*
*They're my parents, my younger brother, and I.*

□ 答對　□ 答錯

　　這三句話的意思是：「有四個。我們有四個人。是我的父母親、我的弟弟，和我。」*There are four.* 可以說成：There are four in my family. （我家裡有四個人。）或 There are four members in my family. （我家裡有四個成員。）

　　*We have four people.* 也可說成：My family has four people. （我家裡有四個人。）或 My family has four members. （我家裡有四個成員。）

　　*They're my parents, my younger brother, and I.* 中的 my younger brother 也可只說 my brother，因為美國人的觀念中，哥哥或弟弟並不像中國人一樣，一定要分得那麼清楚。

　　美國人稱「我的弟弟」為：my younger brother；my little brother；my kid brother。美國人稱「我的哥哥」為：my older brother；my big brother，也有人用 my elder brother，但不那麼普遍。

Question 7

# *What are you doing this weekend?*

（未回答前，勿翻下一頁）

* weekend〔'wik'ɛnd〕*n.* 週末

　這句話的意思是「你這個週末要做什麼？」暗示「你這個週末有什麼計劃？」用現在進行式表「不久的未來」。也有美國人説：What will you do this weekend? ( 你這個週末要做什麼？) 或 What are you going to do this weekend? ( 這個週末你打算做什麼？)

下面都是美國人常説的話：

**What are you doing this weekend?** 【第一常用】
【this 加時間名詞，前面的介詞應省略。】

What are you doing on the weekend? 【第五常用】
( 你週末時要做什麼？)

What are you doing this Saturday and Sunday?
( 這個星期六和星期天你要做什麼？)【第六常用】

What are you planning for the weekend?
( 你週末打算做什麼？)【第三常用】

What are your plans for the weekend? 【第二常用】
( 你週末有什麼計劃？)

What are your weekend plans? 【第四常用】
( 你週末有什麼計劃？)

## Answers 7

*I'm not sure yet.*

*I don't have any plans.*

*What do you suggest?*

□答對　□答錯

---

\* *not…yet* 尚未…　　suggest〔səg'dʒɛst〕*v.* 建議

這三句話的意思是「我還不確定。我沒有任何計劃。你有什麼建議嗎？」也可以回答說：

I have no idea. ( 我不知道。)

I might hang out at home.

( 我也許會待在家裡。)【*hang out* 在～閒蕩；待在～】

It's too early to tell.

( 現在還太早，很難說。)

【這句話源自：It's too early for me to tell you.】

下面三句也是一個好的選擇：

I'll study a little. ( 我會讀點書。)

I'll probably go window-shopping.

( 我也許會去逛街瀏覽櫥窗。)

I might go see a movie.

( 我也許會去看場電影。)

window-shopping〔'wɪndo‚ʃɑpɪŋ〕*n.* 瀏覽櫥窗

*go see a movie* 去看一場電影 ( = *go and see a movie* )

## Question 8

# *Who is your favorite teacher?*

（未回答前，勿翻下一頁）

* favorite〔'fevərɪt〕*adj.* 最喜愛的

這句話的意思是「誰是你最喜愛的老師？」可加長爲：
Who is your favorite teacher in school?（在學校，誰是
你最喜愛的老師？）或 Tell me, "Who is your favorite
teacher?"（告訴我：「誰是你最喜愛的老師？」）

下面是美國人常說的話：

> ***Who is your favorite teacher?*** 【第一常用】
> What teacher is your favorite?【第五常用】
> （你最喜愛的是哪個老師？）
> Which teacher is your favorite?【第二常用】
> （哪個老師是你最喜愛的？）
> 【favorite〔'fevərɪt〕*n.* 最喜愛的人或物】
>
> What teacher do you like most?【第七常用】
> （你最喜歡哪個老師？）
> Which teacher do you like most?【第四常用】
> （你最喜歡哪個老師？）
>
> What teacher do you like best?【第六常用】
> （你最喜歡哪個老師？）
> Which teacher do you like best?【第三常用】
> （你最喜歡哪個老師？）

**Answers 8**

*I like Miss Lee.*
*She's my favorite.*
*She's a wonderful teacher.*

□ 答對　□ 答錯

這三句話的意思是「我喜歡李老師。她是我最喜愛的。
她是個很棒的老師。」

在美國，稱呼老師，通常冠上 Miss 或 Mr.，而不說
*Teacher Lee*（誤）。

*She's my favorite.* 也可說成：She's my favorite
teacher.（她是我最喜愛的老師。）

下面三句也是不錯的選擇：

Miss Lee is my favorite.（我最喜歡李老師。）
She is an interesting teacher.（她教書很風趣。）
She has a nice personality.（她有很好的個性。）
interesting（ˈɪntrɪstɪŋ）*adj.* 有趣的
personality（ˌpɝsṇˈæləti）*n.* 個性

也可以用下面三句來回答：

My favorite teacher is Miss Lee.
（我最喜愛的是李老師。）
Her class is interesting.（她上課很有趣。）
She's fair to everyone.（她對每個人都公平。）
【fair（fɛr）*adj.* 公平的】

Question 9

# *What time is it?*

（未回答前，勿翻下一頁）

這句話的意思是「現在幾點？」可加長為：What time is it now?（現在幾點？）或 What time is it right now?（現在幾點？）比較禮貌的說法是：May I ask, "What time is it?"（可不可以請問：「現在幾點？」）

下面都是美國人常說的話：

***What time is it?*** 【第一常用】

What's the time?（現在幾點？）【第二常用】

What time do you have?【第三常用】

（你知道現在幾點嗎？）

Do you have the time?（你知道現在幾點嗎？）【第六常用】

Do you know the time?（你知道現在幾點嗎？）【第七常用】

Do you know what time it is?【第八常用】

（你知道現在幾點嗎？）

May I ask the time?（我可以請問現在幾點嗎？）【第四常用】

May I have the time?（請問現在幾點？）【第五常用】

Could you please tell me the time?【第九常用】

（能不能請你告訴我現在幾點？）

Please tell me the time.（請告訴我現在幾點。）【第十常用】

## Answers 9

> *Let me see.*
>
> *It's three twenty.*
>
> *It's twenty after three.*

□ 答對　　□ 答錯

這三句話的意思是「讓我看看。三點二十分。現在是三點二十分。」*Let me see.* 也可說成：Let me check. (讓我看看。) 也有人說：Wait a moment. (等一下。)

下面都是美國人常說的話，我們按照使用頻率排列：

① *It's three twenty.*【第一常用】

② *It's twenty after three.*【第二常用】

③ It's twenty minutes after three.【第三常用】
(現在是三點二十分。)

④ It's twenty past three. (現在是三點二十分。)
【past〔pæst〕*prep.* 超過】

⑤ It's about twenty after three. (現在大約是三點二十分。)

⑥ It's exactly twenty after three. (現在正好是三點二十分。)

⑦ It's close to twenty after three. (現在將近三點二十分。)
【exactly〔ɪɡ'zæktlɪ〕*adv.* 正好　*close to* 將近】

下面是「現在是三點十五分。」常用的說法：

It's three fifteen.【第一常用】

It's a quarter after three.【第三常用】

It's a quarter past three.【第二常用】

【quarter〔'kwɔrtɚ〕*n.* 十五分鐘】

**Question 10**

# *How do you do?*

（未回答前，勿翻下一頁）

　　這句話的意思是「你好。」不是眞的問句，而是初次見面的問候語。【詳見「一口氣英語⑤」p.2-4】

下面都是初次見面的人常說的話：

***How do you do ?*** 【第一常用】
How are you? ( 你好嗎？)【第二常用】

Nice to meet you. ( 很高興認識你。)【第三常用】
Good to meet you. ( 認識你眞好。)【第四常用】
Glad to meet you. ( 很高興認識你。)【第五常用】
【meet〔mit〕*v.* 認識　glad〔glæd〕*adj.* 高興的】

Happy to meet you. ( 很高興認識你。)【第六常用】
Pleased to meet you. ( 很高興認識你。)【第七常用】
I'm glad we could meet. ( 很高興我們能認識。)【第十常用】
【pleased〔plizd〕*adj.* 高興的】

I'm happy to make your acquaintance. 【第八常用】
( 很高興認識你。)
How nice to meet you. ( 認識你眞好。)【第九常用】
I'm pleased to make your acquaintance. ( 我很高興認識你。)
acquaintance〔ə'kwentəns〕*n.* 認識　　　　　　　【第十四常用】
***make one's acquaintance*** 認識某人

It's a pleasure. ( 眞是榮幸。)【第十一常用】
It's been a pleasure. ( 眞是榮幸。)【第十二常用】
It's been a pleasure meeting you. ( 認識你是我的榮幸。)
【pleasure〔'plɛʒɚ〕*n.* 樂趣；榮幸】　　　　　　【第十三常用】

## Answers 10

*Hello.*

*How do you do?*

*Nice to meet you.*

□答對　□答錯

這三句話的意思是「哈囉。你好。很高興認識你。」可用 How are you? 來加強 Hello 的語氣，說成：*Hello. How are you?*（哈囉。你好嗎？）

當對方說：How do you do? 你也可以用：*How do you do?* 來回答。

當對方說：*Nice to meet you.* 的時候，你才可以說：Nice to meet you, too.（我也很高興認識你。）來回答。

也可以說以下三句來回答：

Hi!（嗨！）

How's it going?（你好嗎？）

My name is Pat.（我的名字是派特。）

也可接著說：

The pleasure is mine.（這是我的榮幸。）

I'm happy we could meet.

（我很高興我們能認識。）

I've heard a lot about you.（我久仰你的大名。）

　　你光會說，不會寫，可能會漏說 ed 或 s。你自己也許感覺不到，可是外國人聽起來就不舒服。所以，一定要經過筆試測驗的練習，你說出來的話才正確無誤。

1. Question：May I ask your name?

　　Answers：＿＿＿＿＿＿＿＿＿＿＿＿＿＿＿＿＿＿＿＿

　　　　　　＿＿＿＿＿＿＿＿＿＿＿＿＿＿＿＿＿＿＿＿

　　　　　　＿＿＿＿＿＿＿＿＿＿＿＿＿＿＿＿＿＿＿＿

2. Question：How old are you?

　　Answers：＿＿＿＿＿＿＿＿＿＿＿＿＿＿＿＿＿＿＿＿

　　　　　　＿＿＿＿＿＿＿＿＿＿＿＿＿＿＿＿＿＿＿＿

　　　　　　＿＿＿＿＿＿＿＿＿＿＿＿＿＿＿＿＿＿＿＿

3. Question：How are you?

　　Answers：＿＿＿＿＿＿＿＿＿＿＿＿＿＿＿＿＿＿＿＿

　　　　　　＿＿＿＿＿＿＿＿＿＿＿＿＿＿＿＿＿＿＿＿

　　　　　　＿＿＿＿＿＿＿＿＿＿＿＿＿＿＿＿＿＿＿＿

4. Question：Where do you live?

　　Answers：＿＿＿＿＿＿＿＿＿＿＿＿＿＿＿＿＿＿＿＿

　　　　　　＿＿＿＿＿＿＿＿＿＿＿＿＿＿＿＿＿＿＿＿

　　　　　　＿＿＿＿＿＿＿＿＿＿＿＿＿＿＿＿＿＿＿＿

5. Question：What are your hobbies?

　　Answers：＿＿＿＿＿＿＿＿＿＿＿＿＿＿＿＿＿＿＿＿

　　　　　　＿＿＿＿＿＿＿＿＿＿＿＿＿＿＿＿＿＿＿＿

　　　　　　＿＿＿＿＿＿＿＿＿＿＿＿＿＿＿＿＿＿＿＿

6. Question : How many are in your family?

　　Answers : _____

　　　　　　 _____

　　　　　　 _____

7. Question : What are you doing this weekend?

　　Answers : _____

　　　　　　 _____

　　　　　　 _____

8. Question : Who is your favorite teacher?

　　Answers : _____

　　　　　　 _____

　　　　　　 _____

9. Question : What time is it?

　　Answers : _____

　　　　　　 _____

　　　　　　 _____

10. Question : How do you do?

　　Answers : _____

　　　　　　 _____

　　　　　　 _____

　　※ 你寫完後，須訂正答案，將錯誤的地方，用紅筆標出來，
　　　以後説的時候，就不會漏掉了。

**Question 11**

# *Make yourself at home.*

（未回答前，勿翻下一頁）

　　到美國人家作客，他們常會説：*Make yourself at home.*
這句話字面的意思是「使你自己像在自己家一樣。」引申爲「不
要拘束。」或「不要客氣。」可以加強語氣説成：Make yourself
right at home. ( 千萬不要客氣。)【right 是副詞，作「就」解，加強
at home 的語氣，像 right now「就在現在」，即「立刻」。】

下面都是美國人常説的話：

*Make yourself at home.*【第一常用】
Make yourself comfortable. ( 不要拘束。)【第三常用】
Please make yourself at home. ( 請不要拘束。)【第二常用】

Our house is your house. ( 我們家就是你家。)【第五常用】
My house is your house. 【第四常用】
( 我的房子就是你的房子。)
Please do exactly as you please. 【第七常用】
( 想做什麼就做什麼。)
【exactly〔ɪgˊzæktlɪ〕*adv.* 恰好；正是　　please〔pliz〕*v.* 喜歡；想做】

You're to do exactly as you please. 【第八常用】
( 你可以想做什麼就做什麼。)【*be to V.* 可以做…】
If there is anything I can do for you, just ask.
( 如果有任何我能爲你做的，儘管開口。)【第六常用】

## Answers 11

*Thank you.*
*You're very kind.*
*You have a lovely home.*

□ 答對　□ 答錯

這三句話的意思是:「謝謝你。你人很好。你家眞漂亮。」
lovely 主要意思是「可愛的」,在此引申爲「漂亮的」,像 a
lovely flower 就要翻成「漂亮的花朵」。

也可回答:

Thanks.(謝謝。)

I will.(我會。)

Your home is so comfortable.(你的家眞舒服。)

I will. 是 I will make myself at home. 的省略。
Your home is so comfortable. 中的 so 在此作「非
常」或「眞的」解,詳見「東華英漢大辭典」p.3268。

美國人也常這樣回答:

I feel at home already.(我已經感到很自在。)

You have a great place.(你的家眞棒。)

It's very cozy.(非常舒適。)

place 的主要意思是「地方」,在此作「家」解,詳見
「東華英漢大辭典」p.2547。

cozy〔'kozɪ〕adj. 溫暖而舒適的

**Question 12**

# *Can you lend me 100 dollars?*

（未回答前，勿翻下一頁）

　　這句話的意思是「你能不能借我一百元？」比較禮貌的說法是：Could you lend me 100 dollars？用假設法助動詞 Could 表示說話者認為不該問而問，所以比較禮貌。加上 please 就更有禮貌了，說成：Could you please lend me 100 dollars?（能不能請你借我一百元？）

【比較】 lend 是授與動詞，要有兩個受詞，borrow 只接一個受詞：

Can you lend *me 100 dollars*?
　　　　　　間接受詞　直接受詞

Can I borrow *100 dollars from you*?
　　　　　　　　　　受　詞

下面是美國人常說的話：

Do you have 100 dollars *you could lend me*?
（你有沒有一百元可以借我？）

Do you have 100 dollars *I can borrow*?
（你有沒有一百元我可以向你借？）

Would it be OK *if I borrowed 100 dollars*?
（你可不可以借我一百元？）

## Answers 12

**Sure I can.**

**No problem at all.**

**Here you are.**

□答對　□答錯

這三句話的意思是：「我當然可以。完全沒問題。拿去。」

**Sure I can.** 可以說成 Yes, I can. 或簡單地說 Sure. (當然。) 也可以說：OK. (可以。) 或 All right. (可以。)

**No problem at all.** 也可以簡化為 No problem. (沒問題。)

**Here you are.** 也可以說成：Here it is. (拿去。) 或 Here you go. (拿去。)

下面三句話也是不錯的選擇：

Here you are.

Here's one hundred.
(這是一百元。)

Is that enough? (夠不夠？)

Do you need more? (需要多一點嗎？)

如果不想借錢給人家，就可以說：

Sorry, I can't. (抱歉，我不行。)

I'm broke right now. (我現在沒有錢。)

I don't have any extra money. (我沒有任何多餘的錢。)

broke 〔brok〕 adj. 沒錢的　　*right now* 現在
extra 〔ˈɛkstrə〕 adj. 額外的；多餘的

**Question 13**

# *Need any help?*

（未回答前，勿翻下一頁）

這句話的意思是「需要幫助嗎？」源自：Do you need any help?（你需要任何幫助嗎？）也可以說成：Need some help?（需要一些幫助嗎？）【詳見 "The American Heritage Dictionary" p.81】

下面都是美國人常說的話：

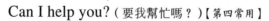

***Need any help?*** 【第一常用】
Need some help? 【第二常用】
（需要一些幫助嗎？）
Need a hand?（需要幫忙嗎？）【第三常用】

Can I help you?（要我幫忙嗎？）【第四常用】
Can I help you out at all?（需要我幫忙嗎？）【第五常用】
Can I help you in any way?【第六常用】
（我可以幫得上忙嗎？）
【***help sb. out*** 幫忙某人　way〔we〕*n.* 方面；方式】

May I help you?（要我幫忙嗎？）【第七常用】
What can I do for you?【第八常用】
（我能爲你做什麼嗎？）
Can I do anything for you?【第九常用】
（我能爲你做什麼嗎？）

## Answers 13

*No, thanks.*

*I got it.*

*I'm OK.*

□ 答對　□ 答錯

　　這三句話的意思是：「不用了，謝謝。我知道該怎麼做。我很好。」*I got it.* 有很多意思，在這裡的意思是「我知道。」或「我知道該怎麼做。」【詳見「一口氣英語①」p.4-4，「一口氣英語⑤」p.7-5】在這裡可以加強語氣說成：I got it. I can take care of it. ( 我知道。我可以處理。) 或 I got it. I can do it by myself. ( 我知道，我可以自己做。) *I'm OK.* 可以加強語氣說成：I'm OK. I'm all right. I don't need any help. ( 我很好。我沒問題。我不需要任何幫助。)

如果你需要別人幫助，就要說：

　　Yes, I do. ( 是的，我需要。)

　　That would be great. ( 真是太棒了。)

　　I could use some help. ( 我有點想要一些幫助。)

　　*could use* 在此作「有點想要」解，其用法在所有字典都沒有，要參考「一口氣英語①」p.5-5，「一口氣英語⑧」p.9-4。

【比較】 下面兩句話，意思接近，句意不同。

　　I could use some help. ( 我有點想要一些幫助。)【較客氣】

　　I need some help. ( 我需要一些幫助。)【較直接】

**Question 14**

# *How was the test?*

（未回答前，勿翻下一頁）

　　這句話的意思是「考試考得怎麼樣？」在美國的隨堂考試稱為 quiz，所以平時考後就可以問同學 How was the quiz?「小考考得如何？」。【quiz〔kwɪz〕*n.* 小考；隨堂測驗】

　　問同學大型考試可以說：How was the exam?「大考考得如何？」其實不論大、小考試，美國人都比較習慣說：*How was the test?* 這句話可以加長為：In your opinion, how was the test?（依你的意見，考試難不難？）暗示「你覺得如何？」所以，從這句話我們可以看出，*How was the test?* 有兩種涵義：①你考得怎麼樣？（= *How was the test for you?*）②考試題目難易度如何？（= *How was the content of the test?*）【*in one's opinion* 依某人之見　　content〔'kɑntɛnt〕*n.* 內容】

下面都是美國人常說的話：

*How was the test?*【第一常用】

How did you do?（你考得如何？）【第四常用】

How did you do on the test?（你考試考得怎麼樣？）【第五常用】

　【do〔du〕*v.* 表現】

Was the test hard?（考試很難嗎？）【第七常用】

Was the test easy?（考試很容易嗎？）【第九常用】

Was the test tough?（考試很難嗎？）【第八常用】

　【hard〔hɑrd〕*adj.* 困難的　　tough〔tʌf〕*adj.* 困難的】

How do you think the test was?（你認為考試怎麼樣？）【第二常用】

How do you think you did?（你認為考得如何？）【第六常用】

How do you feel about the test?（你感覺考得如何？）【第三常用】

## Answers 14

***It was tough*.**

***It was difficult*.**

***It wasn't easy*.**

□ 答對　□ 答錯

* tough〔tʌf〕*adj.* 困難的（= *hard* = *difficult*）

這三句話的意思是：「難，很困難，不簡單。」

對於考試困難，你也可以説下面三句話：

It was a challenge.（它是個挑戰。）

I had a tough time.（我很辛苦。）

I thought it was tough.（我認為很難。）

challenge〔'tʃælɪndʒ〕*n.* 挑戰

tough〔tʌf〕*adj.* 艱苦的　***have a tough time*** 很辛苦

如果考試簡單，你可以説：

It was easy.（簡單。）

It wasn't hard at all.（一點都不難。）

It was a piece of cake.（很簡單。）

【***not…at all*** 一點也不⋯　***a piece of cake*** 很簡單（= *very easy*）】

也可以説這三句，表示考試不難：

It wasn't tough.（不難。）

It wasn't difficult.（不困難。）

I had no trouble at all.（我一點困難也沒有。）

【trouble〔'trʌbḷ〕*n.* 困難；煩惱；麻煩】

## Question 15

# *What did you eat for breakfast?*

（未回答前，勿翻下一頁）

　　這句話的意思是「你早餐吃了什麼？」可以加長為：What did you eat for breakfast this morning?（你今天早上早餐吃什麼？）

下面都是美國人常説的話，第一～三句使用頻率很接近：

*What did you eat for breakfast?*【第一常用】
What did you have for breakfast?【第二常用】
（你今天早餐吃了什麼？）【have〔hæv〕v. 吃；喝】
What did you eat this morning?【第三常用】
（你今天早上吃了什麼？）

I'd like to know what you ate for breakfast.
（我想知道你早餐吃了什麼。）【第六常用】
I'm curious as to what you ate for breakfast.
（我很好奇你早餐吃了什麼。）【第七常用】
Tell me what you ate for breakfast.
（告訴我你早餐吃了什麼。）【第五常用】

What was your breakfast?
（你早餐吃了什麼？）【第四常用】
Did you eat breakfast at home or outside?
（你早餐是在家吃還是在外面吃的？）【第九常用】
Did you eat Chinese or Western food for
　　breakfast?（你吃中式還是西式早餐？）【第八常用】

## Answers 15

*I ate a baked roll.*

*I had a fritter.*

*I drank some soy milk.*

□ 答對　□ 答錯

---

\* **baked roll** 燒餅　　fritter〔ˈfrɪtɚ〕 *n.* 油條
soy〔sɔɪ〕 *n.* 黃豆（ = *soybean* ）　　**soy milk** 豆漿

　　這三句話的意思是「我吃了燒餅。我吃了油條。我喝了一些豆漿。」
baked roll 字面意思是「烘烤的麵包捲」，所以美國人把「燒餅」稱做
baked roll，也有美國人把燒餅稱作 bread，因為和麵包類似。

　　fritter 本來是美國人吃的「帶餡油炸麵糰」，和「油條」有點像，
所以美國人把「油條」稱做 Chinese fritter 或 fritter，也有美國人
稱爲 fried bread roll（炸麵包捲）。soy milk 是「豆漿」，也有美國
人說 soybean milk，但是沒有人說 *bean milk*（誤），因為 bean 的
品種很多，有 green bean（綠豆）、red bean（紅豆）等。

　　這三句話可以簡單說成：I had a baked roll, a fritter and
soy milk.（我吃了燒餅、油條和豆漿。）

如果你吃了「饅頭、稀飯、蛋」，你就可以說下面三句：

I had a steamed bun.（我吃了饅頭。）【 **steamed bun** 饅頭 】
I had some rice soup.（我吃了一些稀飯。）【 **rice soup** 稀飯 】
I also had an egg.（我也吃了一個蛋。）

如果你吃了西式早餐，你就可以說：

I ate a sandwich.（我吃了一個三明治。）
I had some milk.（我喝了一些牛奶。）（ = *I drank some milk.* ）
I also ate some fruit.（我也吃了一點水果。）

**Question 16**

# *What grade are you in?*

（未回答前，勿翻下一頁）

* grade〔gred〕*n.* 年級

***What grade are you in?*** 的意思是：「你幾年級？」也可以加長爲：What grade are you in at school?（你在學校幾年級？）at school 可以說成 in school。像 In school, what grade are you in?（＝What grade are you in in school?）句中的 school 都可改成 your school，像 At your school, what grade are you in?（在學校，你幾年級？）

下面都是美國人常說的話：

***What grade are you in?***【第一常用】
What year are you in?（你幾年級？）【第二常用】
Which grade are you in?【第三常用】
（你哪一年級？）

Tell me, "What grade are you in?"【第四常用】
（告訴我，你幾年級？）
Tell me what grade you are in.【第五常用】
（告訴我你幾年級。）
Can you tell me what grade you are in?
（你能告訴我，你幾年級嗎？）【第六常用】

## Answers 16

*I'm in the third grade.*

*I'm a third-year student.*

*I will graduate this year.*

□答對　□答錯

　　*I'm in the third grade.* 的意思是「我三年級。」也可以說成：I'm in my third year. 或 I'm on my third year. 也有美國人說：I'm in grade three. 意思都相同。

　　*I'm a third-year student.* 意思是「我是三年級學生。」也可以說成：I'm a third-grade student. ( 我是三年級的學生。) I will graduate this year. 意思是「我今年畢業。」

【比較】 下面三句意思相同，前兩句使用頻率接近：

　　　*I will graduate this year.* 【較常用】

　　= I'm graduating this year. 【較常用】

　　= I graduate this year. 【常用】

　　有些動詞句意明確時，可用現在式或現在進行式，表不久的未來。【詳見「文法寶典」p.341】

下面三句話也是美國人常說的：

　　　This is my third year. ( 我現在三年級。)

　　　This is my final year. ( 這是我的最後一年。)

　　　It's my last year. ( 是我的最後一年。)

---

**Question 17**

# *What are your future plans?*

（未回答前，勿翻下一頁）

---

\* future〔ˈfjutʃɚ〕*adj.* 未來的 *n.* 未來

這句話的意思是「你未來的計劃是什麼？」可以客氣地問：May I ask, "What are your future plans?"（我可不可以請問你：「你未來的計劃是什麼？」)

下面都是美國人常說的話：

***What are your future plans?***【第一常用】

What are your plans for the future?【第二常用】
（你未來有什麼計劃？）

What are your future hopes and dreams?【第五常用】
（你未來的希望和夢想是什麼？）

What would you like to achieve in the future?
（你未來想要做什麼？）【第六常用】【achieve〔əˈtʃiv〕*v.* 達成】

What things do you want to do in the future?
（你未來想要做什麼事情？）【第四常用】

What do you want to do in the future?
（你未來想要做什麼？）【第三常用】

In the future, what would you like to do?
（未來你想要做什麼？）【第七常用】

Ten years from now, what would you like to be doing?
（十年以後，你想要做什麼？）【第九常用】

After you finish school, what do you want to do?【第八常用】
（畢業以後，你想要做什麼？）【*finish school* 完成學業；畢業】

## Answers 17

*I want to help people.*

*I want to be useful to society.*

*I want to make my family proud.*

□ 答對　□ 答錯

\* useful〔'jusfəl〕adj. 有用的　　society〔sə'saɪətɪ〕n. 社會
proud〔praud〕adj. 驕傲的；感到光榮的

　　這三句話的意思是「我想要幫助人們。我想要對社會有用。
我想要家人以我爲榮。」連續說三個 I want to...，有加強語
氣的作用，是美國人說話的習慣。

上面這三句話，可以用在面談時。私底下，你可以說：

　　I want to be rich.（我想要有錢。）
　　I want to travel a lot.（我想要經常旅行。）
　　I want a happy life.（我想要快樂的生活。）【*a lot*　常常】

也可以說下面三句：

　　I want to be fluent in English.（我希望英文很流利。）
　　I want to start a company.（我想要開公司。）
　　I want to be my own boss.（我想要自己當老板。）
　　【fluent〔'fluənt〕adj. 流利的　　start〔start〕v. 創辦】

下面三句是不錯的選擇：

　　I want to study hard.（我想要努力用功。）
　　I want to study abroad.（我想要出國唸書。）
　　I want to be an expert.（我想要成爲專家。）
　　【abroad〔ə'brɔd〕adv. 到國外　　expert〔'ɛkspɝt〕n. 專家】

**Question 18**

# *What time do you go to bed?*

（未回答前，勿翻下一頁）

這句話的意思是「你什麼時候睡覺？」可以客氣地說：May I ask, "What time do you go to bed?"（可不可以請問，「你幾點睡覺？」）可以加長爲：What time do you go to bed every night?（你每天晚上幾點睡覺？）或 What time do you go to bed at night?（你晚上幾點睡覺？）

【比較】*What time do you go to bed?*【正】

*What time do you go to the bed?*

【誤，bed 在此是抽象名詞，不可加冠詞】

下面是美國人常說的話：

*What time do you go to bed?*【第一常用】

What time do you go to sleep?（你幾點睡覺？）【第三常用】

When do you go to bed?（你什麼時候睡覺？）【第二常用】

When do you go to sleep?（你什麼時候睡覺？）【第四常用】

Around what time do you go to bed?【第五常用】

（你大概幾點睡覺？）

About what time do you go to bed?【第六常用】

（你大概幾點睡覺？）

At about what time do you go to bed?【第七常用】

（你大概幾點睡覺？）

**What time do you go to bed?** 也常加上 usually 或 often，成爲：What time do you *usually* go to bed?（你通常什麼時候睡覺？）或 What time do you *often* go to bed?（你常常什麼時候睡覺？）

---

**Answers 18**

*About eleven.*

*Sometimes later.*

*It depends on what night it is.*

□答對　□答錯

---

\* *depend on*　視…而定

　　*About eleven.* 的意思是「大約十一點。」源自：I go to bed about eleven. ( 我大概十一點睡覺。) 也常說成：Around eleven. ( 大約十一點。) *Sometimes later.* 的意思是「有時候晚一點。」源自：Sometimes I go to bed later. ( 有時候我比較晚睡。) *It depends on what night it is.* 的意思是「要看哪一天晚上而定。」主詞 It 在這裡是指 My bedtime ( 我的睡覺時間 )。【bedtime〔ˈbɛd͵taɪm〕*n.* 睡覺時間】

也可說下面三句：

　　Around eleven. ( 大約十一點。)
　　I usually go to bed around eleven. ( 我通常大約十一點睡覺。)
　　On weekends, it's later. ( 週末時候晚一點。)
　　【weekend〔ˈwikˈɛnd〕*n.* 週末】

下面三句也是很好的選擇：

　　On school nights, I go to bed at eleven.
　　( 隔天要上課時，我十一點睡覺。)
　　On weekends, I get to bed at midnight.
　　( 週末的時候，我十二點睡覺。)
　　Sometimes I stay up much later. ( 有時候我熬夜熬到更晚。)
　　*school night* 隔天要上課的晚上 ( 從週日晚上到週四晚上 )
　　midnight〔ˈmɪd͵naɪt〕*n.* 半夜；午夜十二點　　*stay up* 熬夜

**Question 19**

# *Good morning.*

（未回答前，勿翻下一頁）

美國人早上見了面，會常說：***Good morning.*** （早安。）來打招呼，有時簡略成：Morning.（早。）或 Mornin' 〔ˊmɔrnɪn〕早。也有美國人說：How are you this morning?（你今天早上怎麼樣啊？）或 How are you this bright morning?（在這個美好的早上你怎麼樣啊？）【bright 主要意思是「明亮的」，在此作「陽光燦爛的」、「晴朗的」解。】***Good morning.*** 的其他說法，詳見「一口氣英語⑨辦公室英語」p.1-3。

到了中午，沒有人說 *Good noon.*（誤）因為中午只要一過 12 點，也許是 0.01 秒，就說 Good afternoon.（午安。）或說 Afternoon.（午安。）到了晚上，天色一黑，就說：Good evening.（晚安。）或 Evening.（晚安。）來和朋友打招呼。

---

**Answers 19**

*Morning.*
*Nice day, isn't it?*
*Have a good one.*

□ 答對　　□ 答錯

---

　　*Morning.* 的意思是「早。」*Nice day, isn't it?* 的意思是「好天氣，對不對？」( = *It's a nice day, isn't it?* ) *Have a good one.* 的意思是「早安。」one 可指 day，morning，afternoon，evening，或 night，在此指 morning。*Have a good one.* 也可作「再見。」解。( 詳見「一口氣英語③」p.4-8 )

也可以回答：

　　Good morning. ( 早安。)

　　I haven't seen you around lately.

　　　( 我最近都沒看到你在附近走動。)

　　How have you been? ( 你近來好嗎？)

　　around〔ə'raʊnd〕adv. 在附近　　lately〔'letlɪ〕adv. 最近
　　See you around. 也可作「再見」講。
　　How have you been? 是 How are you? 的完成式型態。

下一組的回答也不錯：

　　Good morning to you, too. ( 你也早安。)

　　What are you doing today?

　　　( 你今天要做什麼？) 【詳見「一口氣英語③」p.4-8】

　　Are you busy? ( 你忙嗎？)

Question 20

# *What's your favorite food?*

（未回答前，勿翻下一頁）

* favorite（′fevərɪt）*adj.* 最喜愛的　*n.* 最喜愛的人或物

***What's your favorite food?*** 字面的意思是「你最喜愛的食物是什麼？」引申爲「你最喜歡吃什麼東西？」可以加強語氣說成：What's your favorite food in the whole world?（全世界你最喜歡吃什麼？）句中的 food 也可用 dish 或 meal 取代。【meal（mil）*n.* 一餐；食物】

下面都是美國人常說的話：

***What's your favorite food?***【第一常用】
What's your favorite thing to eat?【第二常用】
（你最喜歡吃什麼東西？）
What's your number one favorite thing to eat?
（你第一個最喜歡吃的是什麼東西？）【第七常用】
【number one 加強 favorite 的語氣】

What food do you like best?（你最喜歡什麼食物？）【第四常用】
What type of food do you like best?【第三常用】
（你最喜歡哪一種食物？）【type 可用 kind 代替】

What kind of food is your favorite?【第五常用】
（你最喜歡什麼種類的食物？）
Which kind of food is your favorite?【第六常用】
（你最喜歡哪一種食物？）【kind 可用 type 代替】

What do you like to eat best?（你最喜歡吃什麼？）【第八常用】
What do you like best to eat?（你最喜歡吃什麼？）【第九常用】
【這兩句話只是 best 的位置不同，兩句中的 best 可說成 the best】

## Answers 20

*I like beef noodles.*

*I like pork chops and rice.*

*I also like a chicken leg with rice.*

□答對　□答錯

* beef〔bif〕*n.* 牛肉　　noodle〔'nudḷ〕*n.* 麵
*pork chop* 豬排　　rice〔raɪs〕*n.* 米；飯

*I like beef noodles.* 的意思是「我喜歡牛肉麵。」noodles 一定要用複數形，當主詞就要用複數動詞，像：Beef noodles are my favorite. ( 牛肉麵是我的最愛。) *I like pork chops and rice.* 的意思是「我喜歡排骨飯。」*I also like a chicken leg with rice.* 的意思是「我也喜歡雞腿飯。」

可以幽默地說：

I'm a meat person. ( 我是愛吃肉的人。)

I love to eat meat. ( 我很愛吃肉。)

I love all kinds of meat. ( 各種肉我都很喜歡。)

【*meat person* 愛吃肉的人　　love〔lʌv〕*v.* 愛；很喜歡】

也可以說下面三句：

I love to eat beef. ( 我很喜歡吃牛肉。)

I also love seafood. ( 我也愛吃海鮮。)

Lobster is the best. ( 龍蝦最好吃。)

【seafood〔'si,fud〕*n.* 海鮮　　lobster〔'lɑbstɚ〕*n.* 龍蝦】

## Questions 11~20  問一答三自我測驗 ◀◀

你光會說，不會寫，可能會漏說 ed 或 s，而你自己不知道，
可是外國人聽起來就不舒服。你一定要經過筆試測驗的練
習，你說出來的話才正確無誤。

11. Question : Make yourself at home.

    Answers : _____

    _____

    _____


12. Question : Can you lend me 100 dollars?

    Answers : _____

    _____

    _____


13. Question : Need any help?

    Answers : _____

    _____

    _____


14. Question : How was the test?

    Answers : _____

    _____

    _____


15. Question : What did you eat for breakfast?

    Answers : _____

    _____

16. Question : What grade are you in?

　　Answers : _____

　　　　　　 _____

　　　　　　 _____


17. Question : What are your future plans?

　　Answers : _____

　　　　　　 _____

　　　　　　 _____


18. Question : What time do you go to bed?

　　Answers : _____

　　　　　　 _____

　　　　　　 _____


19. Question : Good morning.

　　Answers : _____

　　　　　　 _____

　　　　　　 _____


20. Question : What's your favorite food?

　　Answers : _____

　　　　　　 _____

　　　　　　 _____


※ 你寫完後，須訂正答案，將錯誤的地方，用紅筆標出來，
　以後說的時候，你就不會漏掉了。

## Question 21

# *Where's the bathroom?*

（未回答前，勿翻下一頁）

---

\* bathroom〔'bæθ,rum〕*n.* 浴室；廁所

　　這句話的意思是「廁所在哪裡？」bathroom 的主要意思是「浴室」，由於浴室裡都有廁所，這個字原來在家裡使用，由於講習慣了，美國人到外面，也把「公共廁所」稱爲 bathroom。「廁所」的說法很多，詳見「一口氣英語③」p.11-8。

　　***Where's the bathroom?*** 也可說成：Where is the bathroom? 在路上問別人廁所在哪裡，比較禮貌的說法是：

Excuse me, where's the bathroom?
（對不起，請問廁所在哪裡？）
Could you please tell me where the bathroom is?
（能不能請你告訴我，廁所在哪裡？）
Please tell me where the bathroom is.
（請告訴我廁所在哪裡。）

　　雖然在廁所上常常看到有 Toilet 或 W.C. 的字樣，但美國人卻不說：*Where's the toilet?*（誤）或 *Where's the W.C.?*（誤）因爲 toilet 含有「馬桶」的意思，W.C.（= *water closet*）是指「抽水馬桶」，美國人認爲這樣說不雅，但英國人卻常用。美國人常用的「廁所」名稱是 bathroom、restroom〔'rɛst,rum〕*n.* 洗手間（= *rest room*）和 washroom〔'waʃ,rum〕*n.* 洗手間。

## Answers 21

*It's down that way.*
*Just go straight.*
*You'll see it on the left.*

□ 答對　□ 答錯

* down〔daʊn〕adv. 向那邊；在那邊　　way〔we〕n. 方向
straight〔stret〕adv. 筆直地　　left〔lɛft〕n. 左邊

*It's down that way.* 的意思是「就在那邊。」down 是用於加強 that way 的語氣。也可說成：It's that way.（就在那個方向。）原則上,「往北」是用 up,「往南」是用 down,現在兩者都可以通用。

It's down that way.

【比較】下面兩句意思相同：

*It's down that way.*【較常用】
= It's up that way.【較少用】

*Just go straight.* 的意思是「只要直走。」也可說成：Just walk straight.（只要直走。）*You'll see it on the left.* 的意思是「你可以看見它在左邊。」也可說成：You'll see it on your left.（你可以看見它在你的左邊。）

也可以說下面三句：

It's down there.（就在那裡。）
Walk down that way.（沿著那個方向走。）
It'll be on your left.（就在你的左邊。）
【down〔daʊn〕prep. 沿著】

（未回答前，勿翻下一頁）

## Question 22

# *What day is today?*

*What day is today?* 的意思是「今天星期幾？」( = *What day of the week is today?* )

這句話不要和 What date is today? 搞混，What date is today? 的意思是「今天幾月幾日？」【date〔det〕*n.* 日期】

下面是美國人常說的話：

*What day is today?*【第一常用】
What day is it today?（今天星期幾？）【第二常用】
What day of the week is today?【第五常用】
（今天星期幾？）

What day is this?（今天星期幾？）【第三常用】
What day of the week is this?【第六常用】
（今天星期幾？）
What's today?（今天星期幾？）【第四常用】

Do you know what day today is?【第七常用】
（你知道今天星期幾嗎？）
Can you tell me what day today is?【第八常用】
（你可以告訴我今天星期幾嗎？）
Please tell me what day today is.
（請告訴我今天星期幾。）【第九常用】

## Answers 22

*It's Thursday.*

*Yesterday was Wednesday.*

*Today is Thursday for sure.*

□ 答對　□ 答錯

* Thursday〔ˈθɝzde〕*n.* 星期四
　Wednesday〔ˈwɛnzde〕*n.* 星期三
　*for sure*　確實地（= *for certain* = *surely*）

*It's Thursday.* 的意思是「今天星期四。」it 可指時間或日期。*It's Thursday.* 等於 Today is Thursday. 也可説成：It's Thursday today. 意思都相同。

*Yesterday was Wednesday.* 的意思是「昨天是星期三。」*Today is Thursday for sure.*（今天確實是星期四。）也可説成：I'm sure today is Thursday.（我確定今天是星期四。）

下面一組也是美國人常説的話：

　　Today is Thursday.（今天星期四。）

　　Yesterday was Wednesday.（昨天星期三。）

　　Tomorrow will be Friday.（明天將會是星期五。）

也可以這樣排列：

　　It's Thursday today.（今天星期四。）

　　Today is Thursday.（今天禮拜四。）

　　Yesterday was Wednesday.（昨天是星期三。）

（未回答前，勿翻下一頁）

## Question 23

# *How do you go to school?*

*How do you go to school?* 的意思是「你怎麼上學？」這句話用現在式表示習慣，可以加上 every day 來加強語氣，成為 How do you go to school every day?（你每天怎麼上學？）

下面都是美國人常說的話：

*How do you go to school?*【第一常用】
How do you get to school?（你怎麼上學？）【第二常用】

By what means do you go to school?【第八常用】
（你怎麼上學？）【means〔minz〕*n. pl.* 方法】
By what means do you get to school?【第九常用】
（你怎麼上學？）

Please tell me how you go to school.【第六常用】
（請告訴我你怎麼上學。）
Please tell me how you get to school.【第七常用】
（請告訴我你怎麼上學。）

Do you walk to school?（你走路上學嗎？）【第三常用】
Do you ride your bike to school?【第四常用】
（你騎腳踏車上學嗎？）
Do you take a bus to school?【第五常用】
（你搭公車上學嗎？）

## Answers 23

> *I walk.*
>
> *My school is in my neighborhood.*
>
> *It's very close to my house.*
>
> □ 答對　　□ 答錯

---

\* neighborhood〔ˈnebɚˌhʊd〕*n.* 附近地區

***I walk.*** 的意思是「我走路。」源自 I walk to school. ( 我走路上學。) 也可以說成：I always walk. ( 我總是走路。) 或 I usually walk. ( 我通常走路。) ***My school is in my neighborhood.*** 的意思是「學校在我家附近。」( = *My school is nearby.* )【nearby〔ˈnɪrˈbaɪ〕*adv.* 在附近】***It's very close to my house.*** 的意思是「非常靠近我家。」( = *It's very near to my house.* )

如果你家住得遠，就可以說：

> I usually take a bus. ( 我通常搭公車。)
> I sometimes take the MRT. ( 我有時候搭捷運。)
> Some days my parents drive me.
> ( 有時候我的父母親會開車載我去。)

some days 在這裡等於 sometimes ( 有時候 )
drive〔draɪv〕*v.* 開車載 ( 某人 )

也可以說這樣三句：

> I ride a bus to school. ( 我搭公車上學。)
> Sometimes my parents take me.
> ( 有時候我的父母親帶我去。)
> My school is far away. ( 我的學校很遠。)

## Question 24

# *When is your birthday?*

（未回答前，勿翻下一頁）

* birthday〔ˋbɝθ‚de〕*n.* 生日

　*When is your birthday?* 的意思是「你的生日是什麼時候？」
當你口試的時候，別人也許會問你：What is your birth date?
（你的出生日期是什麼時候？）或 On what date were you born?
（你是在什麼日期出生的？）

下面都是美國人常說的話：

*When is your birthday?*【第一常用】
What's your birthday?（你的生日是什麼時候？）【第二常用】
On what day is your birthday?【第五常用】
（你的生日是哪一天？）

Can you tell me your birthday?【第六常用】
（你能不能告訴我你的生日？）
Please tell me your birthday.（請告訴我你的生日。）【第七常用】

When were you born?（你是何時出生的？）【第八常用】
On what day were you born?【第九常用】
（你是哪一天出生的？）
On what day of the year were you born?【第十常用】
（你是一年中的哪一天出生的？）

What day is your birthday?（你的生日是哪一天？）【第三常用】
What day is your birthday on?【第四常用】
（你的生日是在哪一天？）

**Answers 24**

*My birthday is in February.*
*It's February second.*
*I was born on February second.*

□答對　□答錯

\* February〔ˈfɛbrʊˌɛrɪ〕*n.* 二月

　　*My birthday is in February.* 的意思是「我的生日在二月。」
*It's February second.* 的意思是「是二月二日。」可説成：My
birthday is February second.（我的生日是二月二日。）等於
My birthday is February the second.

　　*I was born on February second.* 的意思是「我出生於二月
二日。」也可説成：I was born on the second of February. 或
I was born in February on the second. 意思都相同。

下面是美國人常説的話，意思都相同：

*My birthday is February second.*【第一常用】
My birthday is *February the second.*【第三常用】
My birthday is *the second of February.*【第五常用】）

My birthday is *on February second.*【第二常用】
My birthday is *on February the second.*【第四常用】
My birthday is *on the second of February.*【第六常用】

比較正式的説法是：My birthday is on the second day of
February.（我的生日是在二月的第二天。）

Question 25

# *What's the date today?*

（未回答前，勿翻下一頁）

\* date〔det〕*n.* 日期

　　***What's the date today?*** 的意思是「今天是什麼日期？」嚴格地説，是問「今天是幾年幾月幾日？」事實上，只是在問「今天是幾月幾日？」這句話也可説成：What is the date today?（今天是幾月幾日？）但語氣稍強。

下面都是美國人常説的話：

What's today's date?（今天是幾月幾日？）【第一常用】
***What's the date today?*** 【第二常用】

What day of the month is today?（今天是幾月幾日？）【第四常用】
What date is it today?（今天是幾月幾日？）【第三常用】

Do you know what today's date is?【第五常用】
（你知道今天的日期嗎？）
Do you know what date is today?【第六常用】
（你知道今天是幾月幾日嗎？）
Can you tell me what day of the month today is?
（你能不能告訴我今天是幾月幾日？）【第七常用】

I forgot what today's date is.（我忘了今天的日期。）【第九常用】
I can't remember today's date.【第八常用】
（我不記得今天的日期。）
I can't believe I forgot today's date.【第十常用】
（我無法相信我忘了今天的日期。）

*It's the fourth.*

*It's April the fourth.*

*Today is the fourth of April.*

□答對　□答錯

這三句話的意思是：「今天是四日。是四月四日。今天是四月四日。」

下面是美國人常說的話：

*It's the fourth.* 【第一常用】

It's April fourth.（今天是四月四日。）【第三常用】

*It's April the fourth.*（今天是四月四日。）【第五常用】

It's the fourth of April. 【第八常用】

（今天是四月四日。）

Today is the fourth.（今天是四日。）【第二常用】

Today is April fourth. 【第四常用】

（今天是四月四日。）

Today is April the fourth. 【第六常用】

（今天是四月四日。）

*Today is the fourth of April.* 【第七常用】

（今天是四月四日。）

Question 26

# *Have you ever been abroad?*

（未回答前，勿翻下一頁）

* ever〔ˈɛvɚ〕*adv.* 曾經　　abroad〔əˈbrɔd〕*adv.* 到國外

　　*Have you ever been abroad?* 的意思是「你曾經出過國嗎？」可加長為：Have you ever been abroad before?（你以前曾經出過國嗎？）可縮短為：Ever been abroad?（曾經出過國嗎？）或 Been abroad?（出過國嗎？）

下面都是美國人常說的話：

*Have you ever been abroad?*【第一常用】
Have you ever been overseas?【第二常用】
（你曾經出過國嗎？）【overseas〔ˈovɚˈsiz〕*adv.* 到國外】
Have you ever been to another country?【第七常用】
（你曾去過其他國家嗎？）

Have you ever traveled abroad?【第五常用】
（你曾經到國外旅遊過嗎？）
Have you ever traveled overseas?【第六常用】
（你曾經到國外旅遊過嗎？）
Have you ever traveled to another country?
（你曾經到另一個國家旅遊過嗎？）【第八常用】

Have you ever gone abroad?【第三常用】
（你曾經出過國嗎？）
Have you ever gone overseas?【第四常用】
（你曾經出過國嗎？）

## Answers 26

*I sure have.*

*I've been to Hong Kong.*

*I've also been to Japan.*

□答對　□答錯

---

\* Hong Kong〔'haŋ'kaŋ〕*n.* 香港

Japan〔dʒə'pæn〕*n.* 日本

*I sure have.* 的意思是:「我當然有。」源自:I sure
have been abroad. (我當然出過國。) 也可說成:Sure, I
have. (當然,我有。) *I've been to Hong Kong.* 的意思是
「我去過香港。」不可說成:*I've gone to Hong Kong.* (誤)
*I've also been to Japan.* 的意思是「我也去過日本。」

也可以這樣回答:

Yes, many times. (是的,很多次。)

I've been to Thailand. (我到過泰國。)

I've also visited the U.S.A. (我也去過美國。)

time〔taɪm〕*n.* 次數　　Thailand〔'taɪlənd〕*n.* 泰國

visit〔'vɪzɪt〕*v.* 去…逗留;遊覽(某地)

下面一組是否定的回答:

No, I haven't. (不,我沒有。)

Not yet. (還沒有。)【*not yet* 尚未;還沒】

I hope to go abroad soon. (我希望很快就能出國。)

Question 27

# *What's your phone number?*

（未回答前，勿翻下一頁）

\* phone〔fon〕*n.* 電話（= *telephone*）　　number〔'nʌmbɚ〕*n.* 號碼

　　***What's your phone number?*** 的意思是「你的電話號碼是幾號？」源自：What's your telephone number?（你的電話號碼是幾號？）如問別人手機號碼，就說：What's your cell phone number?（你的手機號碼是幾號？）【*cell phone* 手機】

　　***What's your phone number?*** 可以簡化為：What's your number?（你的電話號碼是幾號？）

下面都是美國人常說的話，我們按照使用頻率排列：

① ***What's your phone number?***【第一常用】
② Can I have your phone number?【第二常用】
　　（你能不能告訴我你的電話號碼？）
③ Could you please give me your phone number?
　　（能不能請你告訴我你的電話號碼？）【第三常用】

④ Would you mind if I asked for your phone number?
　　（你介不介意我跟你要電話號碼？）【*ask for* 要；要求】
⑤ Is it OK to give me your phone number?
　　（可以給我你的電話號碼嗎？）
⑥ Is it OK to ask for your phone number?
　　（可以要你的電話號碼嗎？）【mind〔maɪnd〕*v.* 介意】

　　上面七句的 phone number 都可改成 number，使用頻率相同。有些年紀稍大的人喜歡說 telephone number。

## Answers 27

*It's 2381-3148.*

*My number is 2381-3148.*

*Want me to write it down for you?*

□ 答對　□ 答錯

這三句話的意思是「電話是 2381-3148。我的電話號碼是 2381-3148。要不要我寫下來給你？」

***Want me to write it down for you?*** 源自：Do you want me to write it down for you?（你要不要我寫下來給你？）可簡化爲：Want me to write it for you?（要我寫給你嗎？）或 Want me to write it?（要不要我寫下來？）

說這三句話後，可接著說：You can call me anytime.（你可以隨時打電話給我。）

也可以這樣回答：

Sure, you can have it.（當然，可以告訴你。）
Here's my phone number.（這是我的電話號碼。）
It's 2381-3148.（是 2381-3148。）

如果不想告訴對方你的電話號碼，就可以這樣說：

I'm sorry.（抱歉。）
I can't give you my number.（我沒辦法給你我的電話。）
Feel free to call me at work.（可以隨時打電話到辦公室給我。）

【*feel free to V.* 可以隨意⋯　*at work* 在工作地點；在辦公室】

（未回答前，勿翻下一頁）

## Question 28

# *What did you do yesterday?*

What did you do yesterday? 的意思是：「你昨天做了什麼？」可以客氣地問：May I ask what you did yesterday? （可不可以請問，你昨天做了什麼？）或 Please tell me what you did yesterday. （請告訴我你昨天做了什麼。）可以加強語氣說成：What did you do all day yesterday? （你昨天一整天做了什麼？）

下面是美國人常說的話：

**What did you do yesterday?**【第一常用】
Tell me what you did yesterday.【第二常用】
（告訴我你昨天做了什麼。）
I'd like to know what you did yesterday.【第四常用】
（我想知道你昨天做了什麼。）

Can you tell me what you did yesterday?【第三常用】
（你能不能告訴我你昨天做了什麼？）
I'm curious to know what you did yesterday.
（我很好奇想知道，你昨天做了什麼。）【第五常用】
How did you spend your day yesterday?【第六常用】
（你昨天是怎麼渡過的？）

curious（ˋkjʊrɪəs）*adj.* 好奇的；想知道的
spend（spɛnd）*v.* 渡過

## Answers 28

*I stayed at home.*
*I studied and relaxed.*
*I watched a few TV programs.*

□ 答對　□ 答錯

* relax〔rɪ'læks〕v. 放鬆；休息　program〔'progræm〕n. 節目

*I stayed at home.* 的意思是「我留在家裡。」可以說成：I just stayed at home.（我只是留在家裡。）〔just = only〕*I studied and relaxed.* 的意思是「我既讀書又休息。」

*I watched a few TV programs.* 的意思是「我看了一些電視節目。」也可說成：I watched a little TV.（我看了一點電視。）或 I watched some TV.（我看了一些電視。）

也可以說下面三句：

I did some homework at home.
（我在家做了一些家庭作業。）
I went out to eat with my family.（我和家人出去吃飯。）
I watched some TV before bedtime.
（我睡前看了一些電視。）〔bedtime〔'bɛd,taɪm〕n. 就寢的時間〕

也可以選擇下面一組：

I read in my room.（我在房間看書。）
I did a lot of sleeping.（我睡了很久。）
I had a relaxing day.（我渡過很輕鬆的一天。）
〔*do a lot of sleeping* 睡了很久　relaxing〔rɪ'læksɪŋ〕adj. 輕鬆的〕

## Question 29

# *What kind of movie do you like?*

（未回答前，勿翻下一頁）

* kind〔kaɪnd〕*n.* 種類

　　*What kind of movie do you like?* 的意思是「你喜歡看哪一種電影？」(= *What kind of movie do you like to watch?* ) 也可以客氣地問：Please tell me what kind of movie you like.（請告訴我你喜歡哪一種電影。）

下面都是美國人常說的話：

　　*What kind of movie do you like?*【第一常用】
　　What kind of movie do you prefer?【第六常用】
　　（你比較喜歡哪一種電影？）
　　What kind of movie do you like best?【第五常用】
　　（你最喜歡哪一種電影？）

　　What's your favorite kind of movie?【第二常用】
　　（你最喜歡哪一種電影？）
　　What are your favorite kinds of movies?【第四常用】
　　（你最喜歡的電影是哪幾種？）
　　What kinds of movies are your favorite?【第三常用】
　　（你最喜歡的是哪幾種電影？）

　　上面各句中的 kind 都可用 type 來取代，但是使用 kind 約佔 70%，使用 type 約佔 30%。kind 用單數時，movie 就要用單數，像 kind of movie；kind 是複數時，movie 就要用複數，如 kinds of movies。

## Answers 29

*I love to watch movies.*
*I'm a big movie fan.*
*I like all kinds of movies.*

□答對　□答錯

\* love〔lʌv〕v. 喜歡　　fan〔fæn〕n. 迷

*I love to watch movies.* 的意思是「我很喜歡看電影。」
也可說成：I love to go see movies.（我喜歡去看電影。）
*I'm a big movie fan.* 的意思是「我是個超級電影迷。」*I like all kinds of movies.* 的意思是「我各種電影都喜歡。」

如果你喜歡動作片和喜劇片，就可說：

I like action movies.（我喜歡動作片。）
I like comedies, too.（我也喜歡喜劇。）
I don't like scary movies.（我不喜歡恐怖片。）

action〔'ækʃən〕n. 行動　　*action movie* 動作片
comedy〔'kɑmədɪ〕n. 喜劇　　scary〔'skɛrɪ〕adj. 可怕的；恐怖的

也可以說這樣三句：

I like romantic movies.（我喜歡文藝片。）
I like cartoon movies.（我喜歡卡通片。）
I especially like martial arts movies.
（我特別喜歡武打片。）

romantic〔ro'mæntɪk〕adj. 浪漫的　　cartoon〔kɑr'tun〕n. 卡通
especially〔ə'spɛʃəlɪ〕adv. 尤其；特別地
*martial arts movie* 武打片（= *kung fu movie*）

Question 30

# *What do your parents do?*

（未回答前，勿翻下一頁）

*What do your parents do?* 的意思是「你父母親是做什麼的？」
可以客氣地説：May I ask, "What do your parents do?"（可不可
以請問：「你父母親是做什麼的？」）也可直接問對方的父親或母親是做
什麼的，説成：What does your father do?（你父親是做什麼的？）
或 What does your mother do?（你母親是做什麼的？）

下面都是美國人常説的話：

*What do your parents do?*【第一常用】
What do your mom and dad do?【第二常用】
（你的爸媽是做什麼的？）
What do your parents do for a living?【第三常用】
（你的父母是靠什麼維生？）【living（ˈlɪvɪŋ）*n.* 生計】

What kind of work do your parents do?【第六常用】
（你父母是從事哪一種工作？）
What kind of jobs do your parents have?【第七常用】
（你父母是做哪一種工作？）

What's your parents' line of work?【第八常用】
（你父母是從事什麼行業？）
What's your parents' occupation?【第五常用】
（你父母的職業是什麼？）
How do your parents earn a living?【第四常用】
（你父母是如何謀生？）

*line of work* 行業　occupation（ˌɑkjəˈpeʃən）*n.* 職業
*earn a living* 謀生（= *make a living*）

## Answers 30

*My dad is a businessman.*

*My mom is a housewife.*

*She used to be an office worker.*

□ 答對　□ 答錯

---

\* dad〔dæd〕*n.* 爸爸　　businessman〔ˈbɪznɪsˌmæn〕*n.* 商人
mom〔mɑm〕*n.* 媽媽　　housewife〔ˈhausˌwaɪf〕*n.* 家庭主婦
***used to V.*** 以前~　　office〔ˈɔfɪs〕*n.* 辦公室；公司
worker〔ˈwɜkɚ〕*n.* 員工

　　***My dad is a businessman.*** 的意思是：「我爸爸是個商人。」也
可說成：My dad works in a company.（我爸爸在公司上班。）***My
mom is a housewife.***（我媽媽是個家庭主婦。）也可說成：My
mom stays at home.（我媽媽待在家裡。）***She used to be an office
worker.*** 的意思是「她以前是公司的員工。」

可依你父母的情況，選擇下面三句：

　　My parents both work.（我父母都在工作。）
　　My dad is in business.（我爸爸從商。）
　　My mom is a teacher.（我媽媽是個老師。）

如果你父親從事公職，就可以說：

　　My dad is a government official.（我爸爸是個政府官員。）
　　My mom works in a bank.（我媽媽在銀行上班。）
　　She is a manager.（她是個經理。）

government〔ˈgʌvɚnmənt〕*n.* 政府
official〔əˈfɪʃəl〕*n.* 官員　　***government official*** 政府官員
bank〔bæŋk〕*n.* 銀行　　manager〔ˈmænɪdʒɚ〕*n.* 經理

## Questions 21~30　問一答三自我測驗

你光會說，不會寫，可能會漏說 ed 或 s，這些小地方你自己不知道，可是外國人聽起來就會很不舒服。你一定要經過筆試測驗的練習，才會注意到細節。

21. Question：Where's the bathroom?

　　Answers：_____

　　　　　　_____

　　　　　　_____

22. Question：What day is today?

　　Answers：_____

　　　　　　_____

　　　　　　_____

23. Question：How do you go to school?

　　Answers：_____

　　　　　　_____

　　　　　　_____

24. Question：When is your birthday?

　　Answers：_____

　　　　　　_____

　　　　　　_____

25. Question：What's the date today?

　　Answers：_____

　　　　　　_____

　　　　　　_____

26. Question : Have you ever been abroad?

Answers : _____

_____

_____

27. Question : What's your phone number?

Answers : _____

_____

_____

28. Question : What did you do yesterday?

Answers : _____

_____

_____

29. Question : What kind of movies do you like?

Answers : _____

_____

_____

30. Question : What do your parents do?

Answers : _____

_____

_____

※ 你寫完後，須訂正答案，將錯誤的地方，用紅筆標出來，
多唸幾遍，以後說起來就不會錯了。

Question 31

# *What's your favorite subject?*

（未回答前，勿翻下一頁）

* favorite〔'fevərɪt〕 *adj.* 最喜愛的
  subject〔'sʌbdʒɪkt〕 *n.* 科目

*What's your favorite subject?* 的意思是「你最喜愛的科目是什麼？」可以加長為：What's your favorite subject in school?（你在學校最喜歡的科目是什麼？）

下面是美國人常說的話，意思相同，我們按照使用頻率排列：

① *What's your favorite subject?*【第一常用】
② What's your favorite class?【第二常用】
　（你最喜歡的課是什麼？）
③ What's your favorite course?【第三常用】
　（你最喜歡的課程是什麼？）【course〔kors〕*n.* 課程】
【上面三句 What's 可用 Which is 來代替，表示「是哪一個」。】

④ What subject is your favorite?（你最喜歡什麼科目？）
⑤ What class is your favorite?（你最喜歡什麼課？）
⑥ What course is your favorite?（你最喜歡什麼課程？）
【上面三句中的 What 可用 Which 代替，表示「哪一個」。】

　subject 和 course 都表示「科目」，但是 class 除了表示「科目」以外，還含有「班級；課程」的意思。

## Answers 31

*English is my favorite subject.*
*I like English best.*
*It's very interesting.*

□答對　□答錯

這三句話的意思是:「英文是我最喜歡的科目。我最喜歡英文。它非常有趣。」*English is my favorite subject.* 中的 subject,可用 class 和 course 取代。*I like English best.* 也可說成:I like English the best. 副詞最高級,the 可省略。(詳見「文法寶典」p.262) *It's very interesting.* 可說成:It's most interesting. (它最有趣。) 或 It's the most interesting class. (它是最有趣的課。)

下面三句也是好的選擇:

I like English best. (我最喜歡英文。)
English is my favorite. (英文是我的最愛。)
English class is interesting. (英文課很有趣。)
【favorite (ˈfevərɪt) *n.* 最喜愛的人或物】

也可以說下面三句:

English is my favorite class. (英文是我最喜愛的課。)
We have an excellent teacher. (我們有很好的老師。)
Our class is always interesting.
(我們的課總是很有趣。)

**Question 32**

# *Thank you.*

（未回答前，勿翻下一頁）

我們可以把：***Thank you*.** 加長爲：

***Thank you*.**（謝謝你。）
Thank you so much.（非常感謝你。）
I thank you so much.（我非常感謝你。）

I want to thank you so much.（我想要好好感謝你。）
I really want to thank you so much.
（我眞的想要好好感謝你。）
I really want to thank you so much for what you did for me.（我眞的想要爲你替我所做的一切，好好感謝你。）

I really want to say thank you so much for what you did for me.
（我眞的想要對你爲我所做的一切，說聲非常感謝你。）
I really want to say to you face to face thank you so much for what you did for me.
（我眞的想當面對你爲我所做的一切，說聲非常感謝你。）
I really want to say to you face to face, from the bottom of my heart, thank you so much for what you did for me.（我眞的想要當面衷心地對你爲我所做的一切，說聲非常感謝你。）

【***face to face*** 當面　bottom〔ˋbɑtəm〕*n.* 心底；深處
***from the bottom of one's heart*** 衷心地；由衷地】

## Answers 32

*You're welcome.*

*It was nothing.*

*Don't mention it.*

□答對　□答錯

* welcome（'wɛlkəm）*adj.* 受歡迎的　　mention（'mɛnʃən）*v.* 提到

中國人對於回答「謝謝。」，往往說「哪裏，哪裏。」如果回答：*Where, where.*（誤）外國人會覺得很奇怪，外國人常回答 *You're welcome.* 字面的意思是「你是受歡迎的。」引申爲「不客氣。」可加強語氣説成：You're most welcome. 字面的意思是「你最受歡迎。」引申爲「你太客氣了。」

*It was nothing.* 的意思是「沒什麼。」可加強語氣説成：It was really nothing.（眞的沒什麼。）或 It was nothing at all.（完全沒什麼。）*Don't mention it.* 的意思是「不要提了。」可以加強語氣説成：Don't even mention it.（連提都不要提了。）【even（'ivən）*adv.* 甚至；連】

下面三句話也是美國人常説的：

No problem.（沒問題。）

No sweat.（沒關係。）

Any time.（不客氣。）

*No sweat.* 字面的意思是「沒有流汗。」引申爲「沒關係。」*Any time.* 源自 I can help you at any time.（我任何時候都可以幫助你。）引申爲「不客氣。」【sweat（swɛt）*n.* 汗；流汗】

**Question 33**

# *May I ask what you do?*

（未回答前，勿翻下一頁）

    *May I ask what you do?* 字面的意思是「我可不可以問你做什麼事？」也就是「我可不可以請問你做什麼行業？」（＝*May I ask, "What do you do?"*）這句話是對不熟的人所說的，較有禮貌。

下面都是美國人對熟人常說的話：

What do you do? (你從事什麼行業？)【第一常用】
What do you do for a living?【第五常用】
( 你從事什麼工作維生？)【living (ˈlɪvɪŋ) *n.* 生計】

What kind of work do you do?【第六常用】
( 你從事哪一種工作？)
What type of work do you do?【第七常用】
( 你從事哪一種工作？)
【kind (kaɪnd) *n.* 種類　type (taɪp) *n.* 類型】

What's your job? (你做什麼工作？)【第二常用】
What's your occupation?【第三常用】
( 你從事什麼職業？)
What's your line of work?【第四常用】
( 你從事什麼行業？)
【occupation (ˌɑkjəˈpeʃən) *n.* 職業　*line of work* 行業】

## Answers 33

*I'm a student.*

*I'm still in school.*

*I don't have a job right now.*

□ 答對　□ 答錯

* *right now* 現在

這三句話的意思是「我是個學生。我仍然在上學。我現在沒有工作。」

如果你有工讀，你就可以說：

I'm a student. ( 我是個學生。)

I have a part-time job. ( 我有兼差的工作。)

I work a few hours every week. ( 我每週工作幾個小時。)

【part-time〔'part'taɪm〕*adj.* 兼差的】

如果你是老師，你就可以說：

I'm a teacher. ( 我是老師。)

I teach at a junior high school. ( 我在國中教書。)

I teach English. ( 我教英文。)【*junior high school* 國中】

如果你從商，你就可以說：

I do business. ( 我從商。)

I work for a trading company. ( 我在貿易公司上班。)

I'm in the marketing department. ( 我在行銷部門工作。)

*do business* 做生意；從商　　*trading company* 貿易公司

marketing〔'markɪtɪŋ〕*n.* 行銷

department〔dɪ'partmənt〕*n.* 部門

**Question 34**

# *Where are you going?*

（未回答前，勿翻下一頁）

*Where are you going?* 的意思是：「你要去哪裡？」美國人碰到朋友，常說：Hey, where are you going?（嘿，你要去哪裡？）【hey〔he〕*interj.* 嘿】或 I'd like to know where you're going.（我想知道你要去哪裡。）有時可加上 now，說成：Where are you going now?（你現在要去哪裡？）可以接著說：Can I join you?（我可不可以和你一起去？）或 Can I come along?（我可不可以一起去？）【join〔dʒɔɪn〕*v.* 加入；和（某人）一起做同樣的事　along〔ə'lɔŋ〕*adv.* 一起】

下面都是美國人常說的話，我們按照使用頻率排列：

① *Where are you going?* 【第一常用】

② Where are you going to?（你要去哪裡？）【第二常用】

③ Where are you heading?（你要去哪裡？）【第三常用】

④ Where are you off to?（你要去哪裡？）

⑤ What's your destination?（你的目的地是哪裡？）

⑥ I'm curious as to where you are going.
　（我很好奇你要去哪裡。）

head〔hɛd〕*v.* 前往　　off〔ɔf〕*adv.* 離開
destination〔,dɛstə'neʃən〕*n.* 目的地
curious〔'kjʊrɪəs〕*adj.* 好奇的　*as to* 關於

## Answers 34

### *I'm going out.*
### *I'm going to buy some things.*
### *I'll be back in a little while.*

□ 答對　□ 答錯

---

\* while〔hwaɪl〕*n.* 短時間

這三句話的意思是「我要出去。我要去買一些東西。我過一會就回來了。」

也可以說下面三句：

I'm going for a walk.（我要去散步。）
I'm going to get some fresh air.
（我要去呼吸一些新鮮的空氣。）
I'm heading for the park.（我要到公園去。）
*go for a walk* 去散步　　fresh〔frɛʃ〕*adj.* 新鮮的
air〔ɛr〕*n.* 空氣　　*head for* 前往

如果要去買東西，還可以說：

I'm going to the store.（我要去商店。）
I'm going to do some shopping.（我要去買些東西。）
I have to buy some things.（我必須買一些東西。）
【*do some shopping* 買些東西】

如果是要去吃東西，就可以說：

I'm going out to eat.（我要出去吃東西。）
I'm going to get some food.（我要去買點吃的東西。）
Do you want to go with me?（你要不要和我一起去？）
【get〔gɛt〕*v.* 買】

Question 35

# *What would you like to drink?*

（未回答前，勿翻下一頁）

　　*What would you like to drink?* 的意思是「你想要喝什麼？」當你到外國人家作客，或和朋友出去用餐，他們通常會問這句話。

　　比較客氣的説法是：Please tell me, "What would you like to drink?" ( 請告訴我：「你想要喝什麼？」) 或 I'd like to know, "What would you like to drink?" ( 我想知道：「你想要喝什麼？」)【*would like to V.* 想要~ ( = *want to V.*)】

下面都是美國人常説的話：

*What would you like to drink?*【第一常用】
What would you prefer to drink?【第六常用】
( 你比較喜歡喝什麼？)【prefer〔prɪˈfɝ〕v. 比較喜歡】

What do you want to drink? ( 你想要喝什麼？)【第二常用】
What do you feel like drinking?【第三常用】
( 你想要喝什麼？)【*feel like V-ing* 想要~】

What kind of drink do you want?【第四常用】
( 你想喝哪一種飲料？)
What type of drink do you want?【第五常用】
( 你想喝哪一種飲料？)
kind〔kaɪnd〕n. 種類　　drink〔drɪŋk〕n. 飲料
type〔taɪp〕n. 類型

## Answers 36

*I'll have a Coke.*
*I'd like it with ice.*
*I'd like it in a glass.*

□答對　□答錯

\* have〔hæv〕v. 吃；喝
Coke〔kok〕n. 可口可樂 ( = *Coca-Cola*〔'kokə'kolə〕n. )
ice〔aɪs〕n. 冰　　glass〔glæs〕n. 玻璃杯

*I'll have a Coke.* 的意思是「我要喝可口可樂。」美國人不習慣說：*I'll have a Coca-Cola.* (少用) *I'd like it with ice.* (我要加點冰塊。) 也可說成：Please add some ice. (請加一些冰塊。)【add〔æd〕v. 加】*I'd like it in a glass.* 的意思是「我要用玻璃杯裝。」

也可以這樣回答朋友的話：

I'd like a glass of pearl milk tea. (我想要一杯珍珠奶茶。)
I don't want too much sugar. (我不要加太多糖。)
No ice, please. (請不要加冰。)
pearl〔pɝl〕n. 珍珠　　*pearl milk tea* 珍珠奶茶
sugar〔'ʃugə〕n. 糖

　即使是紙杯或塑膠杯，只要是大杯的，都要用 glass，小杯的才用 cup。到店裡點飲料的時候，店員常會問：Do you want a cup or a glass? 意思是「你要小杯或大杯的？」

glass　　cup

**Question 36**

# *Want to grab a bite?*

（未回答前，勿翻下一頁）

---

\*grab〔græb〕*v.* 抓　　bite〔baɪt〕*n.* 一口（食物）

這句話字面的意思是「想去抓一口食物嗎？」可引申為「想要吃一點東西嗎？」源自：Do you want to grab a bite to eat?（你想不想去吃一點東西？）

grab a bite 可以當作成語來看，相當於 eat a light meal（吃點簡餐）或 get a snack（吃點點心）。【light〔laɪt〕*adj.* 少量的 meal〔mil〕*n.* 一餐　　snack〔snæk〕*n.* 點心】

下面是美國人常說的話，我們按照使用頻率排列：

***Want to grab a bite?***【第一常用】
Want to go eat?（想要去吃東西嗎？）【第二常用】

Want to get something to eat?【第三常用】
（想要買點東西吃嗎？）
Want to go and get something to eat?
（想要去買點東西吃嗎？）【get〔gɛt〕*v.* 買】

Want to eat with me?（想和我去吃東西嗎？）
Want to go out for a bite with me?（想和我出去吃點東西嗎？）

Would you like to get something to eat?
（你想買點東西吃嗎？）
Would you like to join me for a meal?（你想和我去吃飯嗎？）
【join〔dʒɔɪn〕*v.* 加入；和（某人）一起做同樣的事】

## Answers 36

*That sounds great.*

*That's music to my ears.*

*That's what I like to hear.*

☐ 答對　☐ 答錯

---

\* sound〔saʊnd〕*v.* 聽起來；似乎
*music to one's ears* 悅耳的聲音；中聽的話

　　這三句話一定要背熟，美國人很喜歡聽。*That sounds great.* 的字面意思是「那聽起來很棒。」引申為「似乎很好。」*That's music to my ears.* 字面的意思是「對我的耳朵來說那是音樂。」引申為「聽起來好極了。」*That's what I like to hear.* 字面的意思是「那是我喜歡聽的話。」也就是「聽起來真棒。」

也可以説下面一組：

I'd love to.（我很想去。）
That would be great.（好極了。）
I could use something to eat.（我想要吃點東西。）
love〔lʌv〕*v.* 喜歡
*could use* 表示「有點想吃（喝等）」【詳見「一口氣英語①」p.5–5】

否定的回答是：

No, thanks.（不用了，謝謝。）
I'm really busy now.（我現在真的很忙。）
How about next time, OK?（下次如何，好嗎？）
　【*next time* 下次】

**Question 37**

# *When are you free?*

（未回答前，勿翻下一頁）

* free〔fri〕*adj.* 自由的；有空的

***When are you free?*** 字面的意思是「你何時有空閒時間？」
(=*When do you have free time?*)【*free time* 空閒時間】也就是
「你何時有空？」是問你個人何時休息，但大部分都是暗示「我
們什麼時候可以見面？」(=*When can we meet?*)

下面都是美國人常說的話：

***When are you free?*** 【第一常用】
When are you available?（你何時有空？）【第七常用】
【available〔ə'veləbļ〕*adj.* 有空的】

When do you have free time?【第二常用】
（你何時有空閒時間？）
When do you have some free time?【第三常用】
（你何時有一些空閒時間？）
When do you have some time off?【第八常用】
（你何時放假？）【off〔ɔf〕*adv.* 休假】

When can we meet?（我們何時可以見個面？）【第四常用】
When can we get together?【第七常用】
（我們何時可以聚一聚？）【*get together* 聚在一起】
When can we spend some time together?【第八常用】
（我們何時可以找時間聚一聚？）

## Answers 37

*I'm free in the evenings.*
*I'm free on the weekends.*
*When do you want to meet?*

☐ 答對　☐ 答錯

---

\* weekend (ˈwikˌɛnd ) *n.* 週末

*I'm free in the evenings*. 的意思是「我晚上有空。」( = *I'm free at night.* ) 也可説成：I'm free every night. ( 我每晚都有空。 ) *I'm free on the weekends.* 的意思是「我週末有空。」也可説成：I'm free on Saturdays and Sundays. ( 我在星期六和星期日有空。 ) *When do you want to meet?* 的意思是：「你要什麼時候見面？」也可説成：When would you like to meet? ( 你想要什麼時候見面？ ) 或 When should we meet? ( 我們應該什麼時候見面？ ) 意思都相同。

也可以説這一組：

I'm free this weekend. ( 我這個週末有空。 )
How about Saturday afternoon? ( 星期六下午如何？ )
Let's get together then. ( 我們到時候見面吧。 )
【then = at that time】

如果想拒絕，就可説：

I'm sorry. ( 我很抱歉。 )
I'm busy all week. ( 我整個星期都很忙。 )
I don't have any free time. ( 我沒有任何空閒時間。 )

---

**Question 38**

# *Where's your favorite place to go?*

（未回答前，勿翻下一頁）

---

\* favorite〔'fevərɪt〕*adj.* 最喜愛的

***Where's your favorite place to go?*** 的意思是「你最喜歡去哪裡？」可以加長爲：Where is your favorite place to go when you have free time?（當你有空的時候，最喜歡去哪裡？）或 Where is your favorite place to go when you want to relax?（當你想休息的時候，你最喜歡去哪裡？）【relax〔rɪ'læks〕*v.* 放鬆；休息】

下面都是美國人常說的話：

***Where's your favorite place to go?*** 【第一常用】
What's your favorite place to go?【第二常用】
（你最喜歡去哪裡？）

Where do you really like to go?【第四常用】
（你很喜歡去的地方是哪裡？）
Where do you like to go?（你喜歡去哪裡？）【第三常用】

Which place do you like to go to the most?【第六常用】
（你最想去哪個地方？）
What place do you like to go to the best?【第五常用】
（你最想去什麼地方？）

Where's a place you really enjoy going to?【第八常用】
（你很喜歡去的地方是哪裡？）
What's a place you really enjoy going to?【第七常用】
（你很喜歡去的地方是哪裡？）

## Answers 38

*I like the park.*

*I enjoy the open space.*

*It's relaxing for me.*

□ 答對　□ 答錯

* open〔'opən〕*adj.* 空曠的　*open space* 空地
relaxing〔rɪ'læksɪŋ〕*adj.* 令人放鬆的

*I like the park.* 的意思是「我喜歡公園。」也可説成：I
like going to the park. (我喜歡去公園。) 或 I like parks.
(我喜歡公園。) *I enjoy the open space.* 的意思是「我喜歡
空曠的地方。」也可説成：I enjoy being in the countryside.
(我喜歡待在鄉下。)【countryside〔'kʌntrɪ,saɪd〕*n.* 鄉下】*It's*
*relaxing for me.* 的意思是「它使我輕鬆。」( = *It relaxes me.* )

也可以這樣説：

Anywhere outdoors. (戶外任何地方。)
I like the mountains. (我喜歡山。)
I love the beach best. (我最喜歡海灘。)
【outdoors〔'aut'dorz〕*adv.* 在戶外　beach〔bitʃ〕*n.* 海灘】

可選擇下面這一組：

I like shopping malls. (我喜歡購物中心。)
I like department stores. (我喜歡百貨公司。)
They are exciting for me. (它們使我興奮。)
*shopping mall* 購物中心　*department store* 百貨公司
exciting〔ɪk'saɪtɪŋ〕*adj.* 令人興奮的

Question 39

# *Where are you from?*

（未回答前，勿翻下一頁）

*Where are you from?* 的意思是「你是哪裡人？」也可說成：Where do you come from?（你是哪裡人？）不要和 Where did you come from?（你是從哪裡來的？）弄混淆。客氣的說法是：May I ask, "Where are you from?"（可不可以請問你：「你是哪裡人？」）(= *May I ask where you are from?*) *Where are you from?* 現在美國年輕人常說成：Where you from?（你是哪裡人？）

下面都是美國人常說的話，我們按照使用頻率排列：

① *Where are you from?* 【第一常用】

② Where do you come from?（你是哪裡人？）【第二常用】

③ What country are you from?（你是哪一國人？）【第三常用】

④ What's your nationality?（你是哪一國人？）【第六常用】
   【nationality〔͵næʃənˈæləti〕*n.* 國籍】

⑤ Where's your home?（你家在哪裡？）【第七常用】

⑥ Where were you born?（你在哪裡出生？）【第五常用】

⑦ Where did you grow up?（你在哪裡長大？）【第四常用】
   【*grow up* 長大】

⑧ Where do you live now?（你現在住在哪裡？）【第九常用】

⑨ Where does your family live?【第八常用】
   （你家住在哪裡？）

```
Answers 39
```

*I'm from Taiwan.*
*I was born in Taiwan.*
*I live in Taipei.*

□答對　　□答錯

---

\* *be born* 出生

*I'm from Taiwan*. 的意思是「我是台灣人。」*I was born in Taiwan*. 的意思是「我在台灣出生。」*I live in Taipei*. 的意思是「我住在台北。」也可說成：My family lives in Taipei. （我家住在台北。）或 My hometown is Taipei. （台北是我的故鄉。）( = *Taipei is my hometown.* )

【比較1】下面兩句意思相同：

　　*I'm from Taiwan*. 【常用，通俗】
　　= I come from Taiwan. 【較少用，45歲以上的人喜歡說】

【比較2】下面兩句意思完全不同：

　　I come from Taiwan. （我是台灣人。）【用現在式表不變的事實】
　　I came from Taiwan. （我從台灣來。）
　　( = *I came here from Taiwan.* )

也可以這樣回答：

　　My home is Taiwan. （我家在台灣。）
　　I was raised in Taiwan. （我在台灣長大。）
　　I'm a native of Taiwan. （我是台灣本地人。）
　　【raise〔rez〕*v.* 撫養　native〔'netɪv〕*n.* 本地人】

## Question 40

# *How do you like this weather?*

（未回答前，勿翻下一頁）

* weather〔ˈwɛðɚ〕 *n.* 天氣

***How do you like this weather?*** 的意思是「你覺得這個天氣怎麼樣？」可以加長為：How do you like this weather today?（你覺得今天這個天氣怎麼樣？）或 How do you like this weather we're having?（你覺得我們現在這個天氣怎麼樣？）

下面都是美國人寒暄常說的話：

***How do you like this weather?***【第一常用】
How about this weather?（這個天氣如何？）【第四常用】
How do you feel about this weather?【第五常用】
（你覺得這個天氣如何？）

What do you think of this weather?【第七常用】
（你覺得這個天氣如何？）
What do you think of this kind of weather?【第八常用】
（你覺得這種天氣如何？）
What do you think about this weather?【第六常用】
（你覺得這個天氣如何？）

Do you like this weather?（你喜歡這個天氣嗎？）【第二常用】
Do you like this kind of weather?【第三常用】
（你喜歡這種天氣嗎？）
Is this weather OK for you?【第九常用】
（你覺得這個天氣可以嗎？）

**Answers 40**

*It's very nice.*

*It feels comfortable.*

*I like it a lot.*

□答對　□答錯

\* feel〔fil〕v. 使人感覺　　*a lot* 非常

*It's very nice.* 的意思是「天氣很好。」It 指「天氣」，也可說成：It's so nice. ( 天氣非常好。)*It feels comfortable.* 的意思是「它使人感覺很舒服。」feel 在「非人」當主詞時，作「使人感覺」解。也可說成：I feel comfortable. ( 我感覺很舒服。)

*I like it a lot.* 字面的意思是「我喜歡這個天氣很多。」引申為「我非常喜歡。」在這裡 a lot 等於 very much。

如果天氣不好，就可說：

It's awful. ( 天氣很糟。)

It's very uncomfortable. ( 天氣令人非常不舒服。)

It's depressing. ( 天氣令人沮喪。)

awful〔'ɔful〕adj. 很糟的
uncomfortable〔ʌn'kʌmfətəbl〕adj. 不舒服的
depressing〔dɪ'prɛsɪŋ〕adj. 令人沮喪的

天氣太熱，就可以說：

It's too hot. ( 天氣太熱了。)

This heat is killing me. ( 熱得令我受不了。)

I don't like this kind of weather. ( 我不喜歡這種天氣。)

【heat〔hit〕n. 熱　　kill〔kɪl〕v. 給 ( 某人 ) 很大的痛苦】

# Questions 31~40　問一答三自我測驗

你光會說，不會寫，可能會漏說冠詞或 s，而你自己不知道，
可是外國人聽起來就不舒服。你一定要經過筆試測驗的練
習，你說出來的話才正確無誤。

31. Question : What's your favorite subject?

    Answers : _____

    _____

    _____

32. Question : Thank you.

    Answers : _____

    _____

    _____

33. Question : May I ask what you do?

    Answers : _____

    _____

    _____

34. Question : Where are you going?

    Answers : _____

    _____

    _____

35. Question : What would you like to drink?

    Answers : _____

    _____

    _____

36. Question : Want to grab a bite?

Answers : _____

_____

_____

37. Question : When are you free?

Answers : _____

_____

_____

38. Question : Where's your favorite place to go?

Answers : _____

_____

_____

39. Question : Where are you from?

Answers : _____

_____

_____

40. Question : How do you like this weather?

Answers : _____

_____

_____

※ 你寫完後，須訂正答案，將錯誤的地方，用紅筆標出來，
　　以後說的時候，你就不會漏掉了。

# *How often do you exercise?*

（未回答前，勿翻下一頁）

* exercise〔'ɛksə‚saɪz〕v. 運動

**How often do you exercise?** 的意思是「你多久運動一次？」

「做運動」的説法還有：work out, do exercise 等。

**How often do you exercise?**【最常用】
= How often do you work out?【常用】
= How often do you do some exercise?【常用】
【**work out** 運動　美國人不用 *take exercise*，只有英國人用。】

下面都是美國人常説的話：

**How often do you exercise?**【第一常用】
How many times a week do you exercise?
（你一個星期運動幾次？）【第五常用】
How much exercise do you get every week?
（你一星期做多少運動？）【第六常用】
【time〔taɪm〕n. 次數】

Do you exercise very often?【第三常用】
（你很常運動嗎？）
Do you exercise a lot?（你常常運動嗎？）【第二常用】
Do you exercise every day?【第四常用】
（你每天運動嗎？）【*a lot* 常常】

## Answers 41

*Not too much.*
*I'm just too busy.*
*I wish I could exercise more.*

□答對　□答錯

*Not too much.* 的意思是「不太多。」源自：I don't exercise too much.（我沒有做很多運動。）*I'm just too busy.*（我就是太忙。）just 用於加強語氣，在此等於 really。*I wish I could exercise more.*（我要是能多運動就好了。）（= *I hope I can exercise more.*）

如果你沒有運動，你就說：

I never exercise.（我從不運動。）
I know I should.（我知道我應該。）
I'm too lazy.（我太懶了。）
【lazy〔'lezɪ〕adj. 懶惰的】

如果你常運動，你就可以說：

I work out every day.（我每天運動。）
I often take a brisk walk.（我常常快走。）
On weekends I like to jog.（週末時我喜歡慢跑。）
*work out* 運動　brisk〔brɪsk〕adj. 快的（= *fast*）
*take a walk* 散步　weekend〔'wik'ɛnd〕n. 週末
jog〔dʒɑg〕v. 慢跑

Question 42

# *I'm sorry.*

（未回答前，勿翻下一頁）

*I'm sorry*. 的意思是「我很抱歉。」可簡化成：Sorry.（抱歉。）
或 So sorry.（很抱歉。）【so〔so〕*adv.* 很；非常地】也可加強語氣說成：

I'm so sorry.（我非常抱歉。）
I'm very sorry.（我非常抱歉。）
I'm really sorry.（我真的抱歉。）

I'm terribly sorry.（我非常抱歉。）
I'm extremely sorry.（我非常抱歉。）

*I'm so sorry.*

【terribly〔'tɛrəblɪ〕*adv.* 非常地　extremely〔ɪk'strimlɪ〕*adv.* 非常地】

*I'm sorry*. 可加長為：I'm sorry about what happened.（我
對於發生的事情感到抱歉。）或 I'm sorry for what I did.（我對於
我所做的事，感到抱歉。）說錯話了，可說：I'm sorry for what I
said.（我對於我所說的話感到抱歉。）也可簡單地說：I'm sorry
about it.（對於這件事我很抱歉。）最囉嗦的說法是：I want to
say I'm sorry to you.（我要說我對你很抱歉。）

除了 *I'm sorry*. 以外，美國人還常說：

I apologize.（我道歉。）
I want to apologize.（我想要道歉。）
I want to offer you my apology.（我想向你表示歉意。）
apologize〔ə'palə,dʒaɪz〕*v.* 道歉　offer〔'ɔfɚ〕*v.* 提供
apology〔ə'palədʒɪ〕*n.* 道歉

Answers 42

*Don't say that.*

*It's OK.*

*Don't worry about it.*

□答對　□答錯

　　*Don't say that.* 的意思是「別那麼說。」相當於：You don't need to say that.（你不需要那麼說。）*It's OK.* 的意思是「沒關係。」可以加長爲：It's OK with me.（我沒關係。）或 What happened is OK with me.（我覺得發生的事情沒關係。）*Don't worry about it.* 的字面意思是「不要爲那件事擔心。」也就是「沒關係。」可簡化爲：Don't worry.（不要擔心；沒關係。）也可禮貌地説：Please don't worry about it.（請不要擔心。）

對於別人所犯的嚴重的錯，你可説：

　　I forgive you.（我原諒你。）
　　It's all right.（沒關係。）
　　I understand.（我明白。）【forgive〔fə'gɪv〕v. 原諒】

下一組也是好聽的話：

　　Forget it.（算了吧。）
　　Don't mention it.（別提了。）
　　It's no big deal.（沒什麼大不了的。）
　　【mention〔'mɛnʃən〕v. 提到　*big deal* 大事；了不起的事】

**Question 43**

# *Good-bye*.

（未回答前，勿翻下一頁）

*Good-bye*. 的意思是「再見。」可以加長爲：It's time to say good-bye. ( 是該說再見的時候了。) 美國人也常說：I have to say good-bye now. ( 我現在必須說再見了。) 或加強語氣說成：I have to be saying good-bye now. ( 現在是我必須說再見的時候了。)

對於熟的朋友，可以說：

> Take care. ( 要保重。)
> Catch you later. ( 以後再見。)
> See you again. ( 再見。)
> *take care* 保重　　catch〔kætʃ〕*v.* 抓到
> later〔'letɚ〕*adv.* 以後

對於初次見面的人，可以說：

> Good-bye. ( 再見。)
> It was nice meeting you. ( 很高興認識你。)
> I hope to see you again soon.
> ( 我希望很快能再見到你。)【meet〔mit〕*v.* 認識】

年輕人可學下面一組：

> Bye. ( 再見。)
> Later. ( 以後見。)
> See ya. ( 再見。)【ya〔jə〕= you】

## Answers 43

*Don't go.*

*Don't leave so soon.*

*Stay longer.*

□答對　□答錯

---

\* stay〔ste〕*v.* 停留

　　***Don't go.*** 的意思是「不要走。」可加長為：Please don't go now.（請你現在不要走。）***Don't leave so soon.*** 的意思是「不要這麼快離開。」可加長為：You don't have to leave so soon.（你不需要這麼快離開。）***Stay longer.*** 的意思是「待久一點。」可加長為：You have to stay longer.（你必須待久一點。）（＝ *You must stay longer.*）

也可以說下面三句，表示你的熱情：

　　　It's too early to leave.（現在離開太早了。）

　　　Don't be in such a hurry.（不要這麼急。）

　　　Stay for another half an hour.（再待半小時。）

　　【hurry〔'hɝɪ〕*n.* 匆忙　 ***in a hurry*** 匆忙的】

如果不想留他，就可說：

　　　OK.（好的。）

　　　Good-bye.（再見。）

　　　See you later.（再見。）

Question 44

# *I like your shirt.*

（未回答前，勿翻下一頁）

*I like your shirt.* 的意思是「我喜歡你的襯衫。」可加強語氣
說成：I really like your shirt.（我真的喜歡你的襯衫。）也有美國
人喜歡說：I like the color of your shirt.（我喜歡你襯衫的顏色。）
或 I like the style of your shirt.（我喜歡你襯衫的款式。）
【style〔staɪl〕*n.* 款式】

*I like your shirt.* 這類的話是美國人的文化，是他們見面時，
常喜歡說的話。除了 shirt 以外，他們也很喜歡稱讚其他東西。

下面是對男生的稱讚語：

　　I like your belt.（我喜歡你的皮帶。）
　　I like your shoes.（我喜歡你的鞋子。）

　　I like your jacket.（我喜歡你的夾克。）
　　I like your pants.（我喜歡你的褲子。）
　　【jacket〔'dʒækɪt〕*n.* 夾克　　pants〔pænts〕*n. pl.* 褲子】

下面是對女生的稱讚語：

　　I like your dress.（我喜歡妳的衣服。）
　　I like your blouse.（我喜歡妳的上衣。）
　　【dress〔drɛs〕*n.* 洋裝；衣服　　blouse〔blaʊs〕*n.* 女用上衣】

　　I like your purse.（我喜歡妳的皮包。）
　　I like your hairstyle.（我喜歡妳的髮型。）
　　【purse〔pɝs〕*n.* 錢包；皮包　　hairstyle〔'hɛr,staɪl〕*n.* 髮型】

## Answers 44

**_Thank you._**
**_Thanks for the compliment._**
**_You really made my day._**

□ 答對　□ 答錯

* compliment (ˈkɑmpləmənt ) *n.* 稱讚
  ***make one's day*** 使某人高興

**_Thank you._** 的意思是「謝謝。」**_Thanks for the compliment._** 的意思是「謝謝你的稱讚。」**_You really made my day._** 字面的意思是「你真的製造了我的一天。」引申為「你真使我高興。」( = *You really made me happy.* )

對於別人的稱讚，也可以這樣回答：

Really? ( 真的嗎？ )
Do you think so? ( 你這樣覺得嗎？ )
I'm glad you like it. ( 我很高興你喜歡。 )
【glad ( glæd ) *adj.* 高興的】

也可以說下一組：

Thanks for noticing. ( 謝謝你注意到。 )
I like it, too. ( 我也喜歡。 )
It's brand-new. ( 它是全新的。 )

notice (ˈnotɪs ) *v.* 注意到
brand-new (ˈbrændˈnju ) *adj.* 全新的

**Question 45**

# *Are you OK?*

（未回答前，勿翻下一頁）

    ***Are you OK?*** 的意思是「你還好吧？」可以加強語氣説成：Are you feeling OK?（你感覺還好吧？）或 Hey, are you feeling OK?（嘿，你感覺還好吧？）【hey〔he〕*interj.* 嘿】也可以多説一句，成爲：You look a little tired. ***Are you OK?***（你看起來有點累。你還好吧？）OK 可用 all right 代替，成爲：Are you all right?（你還好吧？）

除了上面所説過的以外，美國人還常説：

    Is everything OK?【較常用】
    （一切都還好吧？）
    Is everything OK with you?【較常用】
    （你一切都還好吧？）

    Is anything wrong?【常用】
    （有任何不對勁的嗎？）
    Is anything the matter?【常用】
    （有任何不對勁的嗎？）

    wrong〔rɔŋ〕*adj.* 情況不好的；不對勁的
    ***the matter*** 困擾的事；麻煩的事

## Answers 45

*I'm OK.*

*I feel fine.*

*Nothing is the matter.*

□ 答對　□ 答錯

　　　*I'm OK*. 的意思是「我還好。」( = *I'm all right.* ) *I feel fine*. 的意思是「我感覺很好。」可以加強語氣說成：I'm feeling fine. ( 我感覺很好。) *Nothing is the matter*.（沒有什麼不對勁的。）【the matter 是慣用語，當形容詞用，等於 wrong 】

也可以幽默地回答：

　　　Yeah.（是的。）

　　　Why do you ask?（你為什麼這麼問？）

　　　Do I look bad?（我是不是看起來很糟？）

　　　【yeah〔jɛ〕*adv.* 是的（ = *yes* )】

如果感覺不舒服，就可以說：

　　　I'm just tired.（我只是累了。）

　　　I had a bad night.

　　　（我晚上沒睡好。）

　　　I didn't sleep well.

　　　（我沒睡好。）

> Question 46
>
> # *What are your summer plans?*
>
> （未回答前，勿翻下一頁）

　　***What are your summer plans?*** 的意思是：「你夏天的計劃是什麼？」往往暗示「你暑假的計劃是什麼？」（= *What are your summer vacation plans?*）

下面都是美國人常說的話：

***What are your summer plans?***【第一常用】
What are you planning to do this summer?【第六常用】
（你今年夏天打算做什麼？）
What are you going to do this summer?【第四常用】
（你今年夏天要做什麼？）

What are you doing this summer?【第二常用】
（你今年夏天要做什麼？）
What are you up to this summer?【第五常用】
（你今年夏天想做什麼？）
What's going on this summer?【第三常用】
（你今年夏天要做什麼？）【*be up to* 想做　　*go on* 發生】

Do you have any summer plans?【第七常用】
（你夏天有任何計劃嗎？）
Do you have any plans for the summer yet?【第八常用】
（你夏天已經有任何計劃了嗎？）
【yet〔jɛt〕*adv.* 已經】

### Answers 46

*I plan to study English.*
*I'll sign up for classes.*
*I want to improve my speaking skills.*

□答對 □答錯

---

\* *sign up for* 報名　improve〔ɪm'pruv〕v. 增進;改善
skill〔skɪl〕n. 技巧;技能

*I plan to study English.* 的意思是「我計劃學英文。」
*I'll sign up for classes.* 的意思是「我會報名一些課程。」
(＝*I'll register for classes.*)【register〔'rɛdʒɪstɚ〕v. 註冊;報名】
*I want to improve my speaking skills.* 的意思是「我想增進
我的說話技巧。」

如果打算工讀,就可以說:

I plan to earn some money. (我打算賺些錢。)
I'm going to get a job. (我要去找個工作。)【get＝find】
Part-time or full-time, I'm not sure.
(我不確定是要兼差或全職。)

part-time〔'pɑrt'taɪm〕adj. 兼差的
full-time〔'ful'taɪm〕adj. 全職的

如果未確定,就可以說:

I don't know yet. (我還不知道。)
I've no idea. (我不知道。)
It's too early to say. (現在說還太早。)【*not…yet* 尚未…】

Question 47

# *What's your favorite sport?*

（未回答前，勿翻下一頁）

**What's your favorite sport?** 的意思是「你最喜歡的運動是什麼？」可能的含意有：① What's your favorite sport to watch? (你最喜歡看什麼運動？) ② What's your favorite sport to play? (你最喜歡從事什麼運動？)

下面都是美國人常說的話：

*What's your favorite sport?* 【第一常用】
What sport is your favorite? 【第二常用】
（你最喜愛什麼運動？）

What sport do you like best? 【第三常用】
（你最喜歡什麼運動？）
What sport do you like the best? 【第四常用】
（你最喜歡什麼運動？）

What sport do you love best? 【第八常用】
（你最喜歡什麼運動？）
What sport do you love the best? 【第九常用】
（你最喜歡什麼運動？）

Which sport is your favorite? 【第七常用】
（你最喜歡哪一種運動？）
Which sport do you like best? 【第五常用】
（你最喜歡哪一種運動？）
Which sport do you like the best? 【第六常用】
（你最喜歡哪一種運動？）

## Answers 47

### *Basketball is my favorite.*
### *It's a lot of fun.*
### *I love to play it.*

□ 答對　□ 答錯

---

\* basketball〔'bæskɪt,bɔl〕*n.* 籃球
favorite〔'fevərɪt〕*n.* 最喜愛的人或物　　fun〔fʌn〕*n.* 樂趣

*Basketball is my favorite.* 的意思是「我最喜愛籃球。」
( = *Basketball is my favorite sport.* ) *It's a lot of fun.* 的意
思是「它很有趣。」( = *It's lots of fun.* ) *I love to play it.* 在這
裡的意思是「我喜歡打籃球。」( = *I love to play basketball.* )

如果你喜歡棒球，就可說：

I like baseball the best. ( 我最喜歡棒球。)
I love to watch it. ( 我喜歡看。)
I love to play it, too. ( 我也喜歡打。)

如果你不喜歡運動，就可說：

I don't play sports. ( 我不會運動。)
I'm not athletic. ( 我不擅長運動。)
I prefer other outdoor activities.
( 我比較喜歡其他的戶外活動。)

play〔ple〕*v.* 參加（球賽、比賽等）
athletic〔æθ'lɛtɪk〕*adj.* 像運動家的；強壯的
prefer〔prɪ'fɝ〕*v.* 比較喜歡　　outdoor〔'aut,dor〕*adj.* 戶外的
activity〔æk'tɪvətɪ〕*n.* 活動

Question 48

# *Mind if I join you?*

（未回答前，勿翻下一頁）

* mind〔maɪnd〕*v.* 介意
  join〔dʒɔɪn〕*v.* 加入；和（某人）一起做同樣的事

    ***Mind if I join you?*** 的意思是「你介不介意我加入你的行列？」這句話可以和朋友、同學、同事，甚至陌生人説。源自：Do you mind if I join you?（你介不介意我加入你的行列？）如果客氣一點，用假設法語氣，可説成：Mind if I joined you?（= *Would you mind if I joined you?*）

看到朋友要去餐廳、去公園，你都可以説：

Mind if I go with you?（你介不介意和你一起去？）

Mind if I go along?（你介不介意我一起去？）

Mind if I go along with you?

（你介不介意我和你一起去？）

【along〔ə'lɔŋ〕*adv.* 一起】

如果要坐在朋友或陌生人旁邊，你可以説：

Mind if I sit here?（你介不介意我坐這裡？）

Mind if I sit with you?（你介不介意我和你一起坐？）

Mind if I sit next to you?（你介不介意我坐你旁邊？）

【*next to* 在～旁邊】

上面兩組的情況，都可以用 ***Mind if I join you?*** 來取代。

## Answers 48

***Of course not.***

***Please do.***

***Welcome.***

□答對　□答錯

對於 Do you mind～? 的回答，千萬要小心，因為 mind 的意思是「介意」或「反對」，別人問你介不介意，你要用否定的回答，才有禮貌。

***Of course not.*** 的意思是「當然不。」源自 Of course, I don't mind. (我當然不介意。) ***Please do.*** 在這裡的意思是「請加入我的行列。」(= *Please join me.*) ***Welcome.*** 的意思是「歡迎。」源自 I welcome you. (我歡迎你。)

也可以說這一組：

Not at all. (一點也不。)
I'd like that. (我喜歡你加入。)
I welcome your company. (我歡迎你的陪伴。)
【company (ˈkʌmpənɪ) *n.* 陪伴】

對於 Do you mind～? 的回答，通常是否定，但 Sure. 是個例外，是表示「不介意。」

Sure. (當然不介意。)
Come on. (來吧。)
Join us. (加入我們。)

Question 49

# *What's new?*

（未回答前，勿翻下一頁）

　　美國人見了面喜歡說：What's up?（發生什麼事？）
***What's new?***（有什麼新鮮事？）【new〔nju〕*adj.* 新的；
新鮮的】這都不一定真正在問有什麼事，而只是打招呼。
所以，***What's new?*** 也可引申為「怎麼樣啊？」或「你好
嗎？」就像中國人見了面問：「吃過飯沒有？」並不一定真
的要請你吃飯，只是在打招呼。真正問別人有什麼消息，
要說：What's the news?（有什麼新聞？）***What's new?***
的詳細用法，可參照「一口氣英語⑨」p.10–6。

　　***What's new?*** 可加長為：What's new with you?
（你好嗎？）或 What's new with you lately?（你最近
好嗎？）也有美國人說：
What's new with you
recently?（你最近好嗎？）
或 What's new with you
these days?（你最近好
嗎？）【lately〔'letlɪ〕*adv.* 最近
recently〔'risn̩tlɪ〕*adv.* 最近
***these days*** 最近】

Answers 49

*Not much.*

*Nothing is new.*

*Everything is the same.*

□答對　□答錯

---

*Not much*. 的意思是「沒什麼。」源自：There is not much new in my life. ( 我的生活中沒什麼新鮮事。) *Nothing is new*. 的意思是「沒什麼新鮮事。」*Everything is the same*. 的意思是「一切都一樣。」

下一組美國人也常說：

Nothing. ( 沒事。)

Nothing much. ( 沒什麼。)

Same old story. ( 老樣子。)

【*same old story* 老套；老樣子】

也可以告訴別人你的近況：

I got a job. ( 我找到一份工作。)

I'm working part-time. ( 我正在打工。)

I'm working at a restaurant.

( 我在餐廳上班。)

【got 在此等於 found。part-time〔'part'taɪm〕*adv.* 兼差地】

Question 50

# *How long will you be gone?*

（未回答前，勿翻下一頁）

當朋友說：I'm leaving. I'm going out. I'll see you.
（我要走了。我要出去了。再見。）此時，你就可以問他：*How long will you be gone?*（你要去多久？）不論他要去多久，你都可以說這句話，不管是幾個小時、幾天，或幾個月。

下面都是美國人常說的話：

> *How long will you be gone?*【第一常用】
> How long will you be away?【第二常用】
> （你會離開多久？）
>
> When will you come back?【第六常用】
> （你何時會回來？）
> When will you be back?【第五常用】
> （你何時會回來？）
> When will you return?【第七常用】
> （你何時會回來？）
>
> When are you coming back?【第三常用】
> （你何時會回來？）
> When are you returning?【第四常用】
> （你何時會回來？）
> When are you expecting to be back?【第八常用】
> （你預計何時會回來？）【expect〔ɪk'spɛkt〕v. 預期】

## Answers 50

*Not too long.*

*Just a little while.*

*I'll be back before you know it.*

□ 答對　□ 答錯

* while〔hwaɪl〕*n.*（短暫）時間

*Not too long.* 的意思是「不會太久。」在這裡源自：I will not be gone too long.（我不會離開太久。）*Just a little while.* 的意思是「只是一會兒。」在此源自：I'll be gone for just a little while.（我只會離開一會兒。）*I'll be back before you know it.* 的意思是「我會立刻回來。」*before you know it* 是一個成語，意思是「幾乎立刻」（= *almost immediately*），說這句話有幽默的味道。

如果離開幾個小時，就可以回答：

Just a few hours.（只有幾個小時。）
I won't be gone long.（我不會去很久。）
I'll be back later.（我待會就會回來。）
【later〔'letɚ〕*adv.* 待會】

如果去渡週末，就可以說：

I'll be gone two days.（我會離開兩天。）
I'll be back Sunday night.（我星期天晚上就回來。）
It's just for the weekend.（只是週末不在。）
【weekend〔'wik'ɛnd〕*n.* 週末】

**Questions 41~50**　問一答三自我測驗

背英文背到最後，往往會忘記細節的部份，像複數的 s 或過去式的 ed，漏說自己不覺得，外國人聽起來會不舒服，所以一定要默寫。

41. Question : How often do you exercise?

　　Answers : _____

　　_____

　　_____

42. Question : I'm sorry.

　　Answers : _____

　　_____

　　_____

43. Question : Good-bye.

　　Answers : _____

　　_____

　　_____

44. Question : I like your shirt.

　　Answers : _____

　　_____

　　_____

45. Question : Are you OK?

　　Answers : _____

　　_____

　　_____

46. Question : What are your summer plans?

Answers : _____

_____

_____

47. Question : What's your favorite sport?

Answers : _____

_____

_____

48. Question : Mind if I join you?

Answers : _____

_____

_____

49. Question : What's new?

Answers : _____

_____

_____

50. Question : How long will you be gone?

Answers : _____

_____

_____

※ 你寫完後，須訂正答案，將錯誤的地方，用紅筆標出來，
以後說的時候，你就不會漏掉了。

## Question 51

# *What do you want to do?*

（未回答前，勿翻下一頁）

美國的小孩在一起時，常說：***What do you want to do?***
意思是「你想要做什麼？」也常說成：What do you wanna
do? ( 你想要做什麼？ )【wanna 〔'wɑnə 〕v. 想要 ( = *want to* )】
往往加上時間，成為：What do you want to do today?
( 你今天要做什麼？ ) 或 What do you want to do after
school today? ( 今天放學後你想做什麼？ ) 他們也常說：
What do you want to do right now? ( 你現在想做什麼？ )
【***right now*** 現在】

下面都是美國人常說的話：

> ***What do you want to do?*** 【第一常用】
> What do you think you want to do? 【第四常用】
> ( 你認為你想要做什麼？ )
>
> What do you feel like doing? 【第三常用】
> ( 你想要做什麼？ )【*feel like* + *V-ing* 想要~ 】
> What would you like to do? 【第二常用】
> ( 你想要做什麼？ )

## Answers 51

*I'm a little hungry.*

*I feel like a bite.*

*I want to get something to eat.*

□答對　□答錯

　　*I'm a little hungry.* 的意思是「我有一點餓。」*I feel like a bite.* 的意思是「我想要吃一點東西。」bite〔baɪt〕*n.* （一口）食物，引申為「一點食物」。feel like（想要），後面可加名詞或動名詞。*I feel like a bite.* 也可説成：I feel like getting a bite. 或 I feel like grabbing a bite. 意思都相同。【grab〔græb〕*v.* 抓】*I want to get something to eat.* 的意思是「我想找點東西吃。」get 在此等於 find。

不知道想做什麽，就可以説：

　　I don't know.（我不知道。）

　　I have no idea.（我不知道。）

　　I'll let you decide.（我要讓你來決定。）

如果你想休息，你就可以説：

　　I'm a little tired.（我有一點疲倦。）

　　I think I'll take a rest.（我想我會休息一下。）

　　I think I'll take a nap.（我想我會小睡一下。）

　　*take a rest*　休息一下　　nap〔næp〕*n.* 小睡

　　*take a nap*　小睡片刻

## Question 52

# *May I ask you a question?*

（未回答前，勿翻下一頁）

　　*May I ask you a question?* 的意思是「我可不可以問你一個問題？」也可說成：May I ask a question?（我可不可以問一個問題？）May 可用 Can 取代，成爲：Can I ask a question?（我可不可以問一個問題？）或 Can I ask you a question?（我可不可以問你一個問題？）

　　也有美國人說：Can I ask you something?（我可不可以問你一些事？）或 Can I ask you about something?（我可不可以問你一些事？）

　　禮貌的說法是：Excuse me, sir. *May I ask you a question?*（對不起，先生，我能不能問你一個問題？）更禮貌的說法是：Excuse me, sir. I hope you don't mind. *May I ask you a question?*（對不起，先生。我希望你不會介意。我可不可以問你一個問題？）

　　也可說成一句，成爲：Do you mind if I ask you a question? 或 Would you mind if I ask you a question? 兩句話的意思都是「你介不介意我問你一個問題？」也可說成：Would you mind answering a question for me?（你介不介意回答我一個問題？）【mind〔maɪnd〕v. 介意】

---

### Answers 52

> *Sure.*
> *Ask me anything.*
> *I'm all ears.*

□ 答對　□ 答錯

---

　　這三句話的意思是「當然。問我任何問題。我洗耳恭聽。」
be all ears 是個成語，意思是「專心聽」。

也可這樣回答：

　　Of course you may. ( 你當然可以。 )
　　Go ahead. ( 儘管問。 )
　　What is it? ( 什麼事？ )

不想回答別人的問題，就可以說：

　　It depends. ( 要看情形。 )
　　Don't get personal. ( 不要問私人的問題。 )
　　Please respect my privacy. ( 請尊重我的隱私權。 )

　　depend〔dɪˋpɛnd〕v. 視情況而定
　　personal〔ˋpɝsn̩l〕adj. 私人的　　respect〔rɪˋspɛkt〕v. 尊重
　　privacy〔ˋpraɪvəsɪ〕n. 隱私（權）

下一組也是好的選擇：

　　Yes, you may. ( 是的，你可以。 )
　　Of course, you can. ( 當然，你能夠。 )
　　Shoot. ( 趕快說。 )【shoot〔ʃut〕v. 說出】
　　【of course 後面的逗點可省略】

Question 53

# *What's your favorite fruit?*

（未回答前，勿翻下一頁）

* favorite〔ˈfevərɪt〕*adj.* 最喜愛的

***What's your favorite fruit?*** 的字面意思是「什麼是你最喜愛的水果？」也就是「你最喜歡什麼水果？」可加強語氣說成：What's your favorite kind of fruit? 或 What's your favorite type of fruit? 意思都是「你最喜歡哪一種水果？」【type〔taɪp〕*n.* 種類】

下面都是美國人常說的話：

***What's your favorite fruit?***【第一常用】
What fruit do you like best?【第三常用】
（你最喜歡什麼水果？）
What fruit do you like the best?【第二常用】
（你最喜歡什麼水果？）

Which fruit is your favorite?【第四常用】
（你最喜歡什麼水果？）
What fruit is your favorite?【第五常用】
（你最喜歡什麼水果？）

Do you have a favorite fruit?【第七常用】
（你有最喜歡的水果嗎？）
Please tell me your favorite fruit.【第六常用】
（請告訴我你最喜歡的水果。）

## Answers 53

*I like mangoes best.*
*I also like litchis.*
*Papaya is delicious, too.*

□ 答對　□ 答錯

* mango〔'mæŋgo〕*n.* 芒果　litchi〔'litʃi〕*n.* 荔枝
papaya〔pə'paɪə〕*n.* 木瓜

這三句話的意思是「我最喜歡芒果。我也喜歡荔枝。木瓜也好吃。」

如果你什麼水果都喜歡，你可以說：

I like too many. ( 我喜歡太多水果了。)
It's hard to answer. ( 很難回答。)
I think most fruit is delicious.
( 我覺得大部份的水果都好吃。)

你最喜歡蘋果，你可以說：

Apples are my favorite. ( 蘋果是我的最愛。)
Watermelon is second. ( 西瓜第二。)
I also like pineapple. ( 我也喜歡鳳梨。)
watermelon〔'wɔtə,mɛlən〕*n.* 西瓜
pineapple〔'paɪn,æpḷ〕*n.* 鳳梨

你最喜歡香蕉，就可以說：

Bananas are my favorite. ( 香蕉是我的最愛。)
I like strawberries, too. ( 我也喜歡草莓。)
Guavas are also great. ( 芭樂也很棒。)
strawberry〔'strɔ,bɛrɪ〕*n.* 草莓　guava〔'gwɑvə〕*n.* 芭樂

**Question 54**

# *Did you sleep well?*

（未回答前，勿翻下一頁）

美國人在朋友間、同學間，或同事間，早晨見面的時候，除了常說：Good morning.（早安。）之外，常問：*Did you sleep well?* 意思是「你睡得好不好？」常簡化爲：Sleep well last night?（昨晚睡得好不好？）或加長爲：Did you sleep well last night?（你昨天晚上睡得好不好？）

Did you sleep well?

下面是美國人常說的話，我們按照使用頻率排列：

① *Did you sleep well?* 【第一常用】

② Did you have a good sleep?【第二常用】
（你睡得好嗎？）

③ Did you have a good night's sleep?【第三常用】
（你晚上睡得好嗎？）

④ How was your night?【第四常用】
（你晚上睡得如何？）

⑤ How did you sleep last night?【第五常用】
（你昨天晚上睡得如何？）

## Answers 54

*Yes*, *I did*.
*I slept well*.
*I got a good night's sleep*.

□ 答對　　□ 答錯

這三句話在這裡的意思是「是的。我睡得很好。我晚上睡了一個好覺。」

也可以這樣回答：

Pretty good. ( 很好。)
I slept seven hours. ( 我睡了七個小時。)
That's enough for me. ( 對我而言已經足夠了。)
【pretty (ˈprɪtɪ ) *adv.* 非常】

如果你睡不好，就可以說：

No, I didn't. ( 不，我沒睡好。)
I didn't sleep well. ( 我沒有睡好。)
I tossed and turned all night. ( 我整晚輾轉難眠。)
【*toss and turn*　輾轉反側】

這樣回答也很幽默：

I had an awful night. ( 我晚上睡得很糟糕。)
I couldn't get to sleep. ( 我睡不著。)
I felt exhausted today. ( 我今天覺得筋疲力盡。)
awful (ˈɔful ) *adj.* 糟糕的　　*get to sleep*　睡著
exhausted ( ɪgˈzɔstɪd ) *adj.* 筋疲力盡的

**Question 55**

# *Can you swim?*

（未回答前，勿翻下一頁）

    ***Can you swim?*** 的意思是「你會不會游泳？」可以加長為：Can you swim at all?（你會不會游一點泳？）( = *Can you swim a little bit?*）或 Can you swim very well?（你是不是很會游泳？）

下面是美國人常說的話：

***Can you swim?***【第一常用】

Do you know how to swim?

（你知道如何游泳嗎？）【第三常用】

Are you a good swimmer?

（你很會游泳嗎？）【第二常用】

【swimmer〔'swɪmɚ〕*n.* 游泳者】

Have you learned to swim?【第七常用】

（你學過游泳嗎？）

Have you ever learned to swim?【第六常用】

（你曾學過游泳嗎？）【ever〔'ɛvɚ〕*adv.* 曾經】

Do you like to swim?（你喜歡游泳嗎？）【第四常用】

Do you swim a lot?（你常常游泳嗎？）【第五常用】

【*a lot* 常常】

### Answers 55

*I can swim a little.*
*I never took lessons.*
*I'm not a strong swimmer.*

□ 答對    □ 答錯

*I can swim a little*. 的意思是「我會游一點。」( = *I can swim a bit.* ) *I never took lessons*. 的意思是「我從來沒上過課。」( = *I never had swimming classes.* ) *I'm not a strong swimmer*. ( 我不是游泳高手。) ( = *I'm not a good swimmer.* )【strong 在此作「精通的；擅長的」解】

如果你很會游泳，就可以說：

   I'm OK. ( 我還可以。)
   I'm a pretty good swimmer. ( 我很會游泳。)
   I swim a lot during the summer.
   ( 我夏天常游泳。)
   【pretty ('prɪtɪ ) *adv.* 相當】

如果你不太會游泳，就可以說：

   No, I can't. ( 不，我不會。)
   I'm not good at all. ( 我游得一點都不好。)
   I'm an awful swimmer. ( 我游得很糟糕。)
   【*not…at all* 一點也不…    awful ('ɔful ) *adj.* 糟糕的】

---

**Question 56**

# *How many languages can you speak?*

（未回答前，勿翻下一頁）

---

　　美國人看到你會說英文，也許會問你：***How many languages can you speak?*** 意思是「你會講幾種語言？」

【language〔ˈlæŋgwɪdʒ〕*n.* 語言】可以加長為：How many different languages can you speak?（你可以說幾種不同的語言？）或 I'd like to know, "How many different languages can you speak?"（我想知道，「你會說幾種不同的語言？」）也有美國人說：I'm curious as to how many languages you can speak.（我很想知道你能說幾種語言。）

【curious〔ˈkjʊrɪəs〕*adj.* 好奇的；想知道的　*as to* 關於】

下面都是美國人常說的話，我們按照使用頻率排列：

① ***How many languages can you speak?***【第一常用】

② How many languages can you speak well?
　　（你會說幾種語言？）【第二常用】

③ How many languages can you speak fluently?
　　（你會流利地說幾種語言？）【第三常用】
　　【fluently〔ˈfluəntlɪ〕*adv.* 流利地】

④ What languages can you speak?
　　（你會說什麼語言？）

⑤ What different languages can you speak?
　　（你會說什麼不同的語言？）

## Answers 56

*I can speak two.*
*I can speak Chinese and English.*
*But my English is not very good.*

□ 答對　□ 答錯

*I can speak two.* 在這裡的意思是「我會說兩種語言。」（= *I can speak two languages.*）*I can speak Chinese and English.* 的意思是「我會說中文和英文。」*But my English is not very good.* 的意思是「但是我的英文不怎麼好。」But 在此是轉承語，連接前面兩個句子。這句話也可說成：But my English is really poor.（但是我的英文真的很糟糕。）【poor〔pur〕*adj.* 差勁的】

可以簡單地回答說：

Only two.（只有兩種。）
Chinese and English.（中文和英文。）
I don't know any other language.（我不懂其他語言。）
　【在此 language 可用單、複數形式】

也可以這樣回答：

I can only speak one language well.
　（我只有一種語言說得好。）
I'm fluent in Chinese.（我中文很流利。）
I can speak a little English.（我會說一點英文。）
　【fluent〔'fluənt〕*adj.* 流利的】

**Question 57**

# *How many are in your class?*

（未回答前，勿翻下一頁）

*How many are in your class?* 的意思是「你班上有多少人？」源自：How many students are there in your class?（你班上有多少個學生？）也可說成：How many students are in your class?（在你班上有多少個學生？）your class 可說成 your school class，成為：How many students are in your school class?（在你學校班上有多少個學生？）

下面都是美國人常說的話，我們按照使用頻率排列：

① *How many are in your class?*【第一常用】
② How many kids are in your class?【第二常用】
　（你們班上有多少個孩子？）【kid〔kɪd〕*n.* 小孩】

③ How many classmates do you have?
　（你有多少個同班同學？）【第三常用】
④ How many boys and girls are in your class?
　（你們班上有多少個男孩和女孩？）
⑤ How many fellow students are in your class?
　（你們班上有多少個同學？）

classmate〔ˈklæsˌmet〕*n.* 同班同學
fellow〔ˈfɛlo〕*adj.* 同類的　　*fellow student* 同學

## Answers 57

*There are thirty-five.*
*My class has thirty-five kids.*
*I have thirty-four classmates.*

□答對　□答錯

　　*There are thirty-five.* 的意思是「有三十五個。」在這裡
等於 There are thirty-five students.（有三十五個學生。）
*My class has thirty-five kids.* 的意思是「我的班上有三十五
個小孩。」也可說成：My class has thirty-five students.
（我的班上有三十五個學生。）*I have thirty-four classmates.*
的意思是「我有三十四個同班同學。」

可以簡單地說：

　　About thirty-five.（大約三十五個。）
　　Almost thirty-five.（幾乎三十五個。）
　　Close to thirty-five.（接近三十五個。）
　　【almost〔'ɔl,most〕*adv.* 幾乎　　*close to* 接近】

也可這樣說：

　　We have thirty-five kids.（我們有三十五個小孩。）
　　Altogether we have thirty-five.
　　（我們總共有三十五個。）
　　There are thirty-five in my class.
　　（我的班上有三十五個。）
　　【altogether〔,ɔltə'gɛðɚ〕*adv.* 總共】

**Question 58**

# *Can you play any instruments?*

（未回答前，勿翻下一頁）

*Can you play any instruments?* 的意思是「你會不會彈任何樂器？」( = *Can you play any musical instruments?* )【instrument (ˈɪnstrəmənt) *n.* 樂器 ( = *musical instrument* )】也可說成：Do you know how to play any instruments? ( 你懂不懂彈任何樂器？)

下面都是美國人常說的話，我們按照使用頻率排列：

① *Can you play any instruments?*【第一常用】
② Can you play an instrument?【第二常用】
   ( 你會不會彈樂器？)
③ Can you play anything?【第三常用】
   ( 你會彈任何東西嗎？)

④ Can you play the piano?
   ( 你會不會彈鋼琴？)
⑤ Can you play the violin?
   ( 你會不會拉小提琴？)
⑥ Can you play the guitar?
   ( 你會不會彈吉他？)

【violin (ˌvaɪəˈlɪn) *n.* 小提琴    guitar (gɪˈtɑr) *n.* 吉他】

## Answers 58

*No, I can't.*

*I can't play anything.*

*I never had a chance to learn.*

□答對　□答錯

這三句話的意思是「不，我不會。我什麼也不會彈。我從來都沒有機會學。」

也可以這樣說：

I can't play any instrument. ( 我不會彈任何樂器。)

I wish I could. ( 要是能夠就好了。)

I wish I could play the guitar.

( 真希望我能夠彈吉他。)

如果你會彈鋼琴，你就可以說：

Yes, I can. ( 是的，我會。)

I can play the piano. ( 我會彈鋼琴。)

I studied the piano for two years.

( 我學了兩年鋼琴。)

也可謙虛地說：

I can play a little piano. ( 我會彈一點鋼琴。)

I took piano lessons. ( 我上過鋼琴課。)

I'm not very good, though. ( 不過我不是很精通。)

take〔tek〕*v.* 上（課）　　good〔gud〕*adj.* 精通的；擅長的

though〔ðo〕*adv.* 不過

## Question 59

# *Do you like learning English?*

（未回答前，勿翻下一頁）

***Do you like learning English?*** 的意思是「你喜不喜歡學英文？」like 後面也可接不定詞，說成：Do you like to study English? 兩者使用頻率和意思相同。可加強為：Do you like learning English at your school? ( 你在學校裡喜不喜歡學英文？ )

下面都是美國人常說的話：

Do you like English? ( 你喜不喜歡英文？ )【第一常用】
***Do you like learning English?*** 【第二常用】
Do you like studying English? 【第三常用】
( 你喜不喜歡學英文？ )【study〔'stʌdɪ〕v. 學習；研讀】

Do you enjoy English? ( 你喜不喜歡英文？ )【第六常用】
Do you enjoy learning English? 【第七常用】
( 你喜不喜歡學英文？ )
Do you enjoy studying English? 【第八常用】
( 你喜不喜歡學英文？ )【enjoy〔ɪn'dʒɔɪ〕v. 喜歡】

Do you like English class? 【第四常用】
( 你喜不喜歡英文課？ )
Do you enjoy English class? 【第五常用】
( 你喜不喜歡英文課？ )

---

### Answers 59

> *Yes, I do.*
> *It's very interesting.*
> *It's my favorite class.*

□答對　□答錯

---

這三句話在這裡的意思是「是的，我喜歡。它很有趣。它是我最喜愛的課。」

也可以這樣回答：

Yeah, I like English.（是的，我喜歡英文。）

Learning English is fun.（學英文很有趣。）

I enjoy speaking English.（我喜歡說英文。）

【yeah〔jɛ〕*adv.* 是的（= *yes*）】

如果你很喜歡英文，就可以這樣回答：

I love studying English.（我很喜歡學英文。）

My English teacher is great.（我的英文老師很棒。）

What we learn is useful.（我們所學的很有用。）

【useful〔'jusfəl〕*adj.* 有用的】

可以簡單回答：

I sure do.（我當然喜歡。）

It's very useful.（很有用。）

It's important for the future.（它對未來很重要。）

【sure 在此是副詞，表示「當然」，不可說成 *surely*】

---

**Question 60**

# *What did you eat last night?*

（未回答前，勿翻下一頁）

---

**What did you eat last night?** 的意思是「你昨天晚上吃什麼？」可以加長為：I'm curious as to what you ate last night. （我想知道你昨晚吃什麼。）【curious (ˈkjʊrɪəs) adj. 好奇的；想知道的 as to 關於】或 I'd like to know what you ate last night. （我想知道你昨晚吃什麼。）

下面是美國人常說的話，我們按照使用頻率排列：

① **What did you eat last night?** 【第一常用】

② What did you have last night? 【第二常用】
（你昨天晚上吃什麼？）【have (hæv) v. 吃；喝】

③ What was your dinner last night? 【第三常用】
（你昨天晚餐吃什麼？）

④ What did you eat for dinner last night?
（你昨天晚上晚餐吃什麼？）

⑤ What did you have for dinner last night?
（你昨天晚上晚餐吃什麼？）

以上兩句的 dinner，可用 supper 代換。在字典上，dinner 是大餐（main meal eaten in the evening），supper 是簡單的晚餐（a light evening meal）。事實上，現在百分之八十的人說 dinner，只有在美國中西部鄉下，較多人說 supper，但如果你說：What did you eat for supper last night?（你昨天晚上晚餐吃什麼？）外國人聽到也不會覺得奇怪。

## Answers 60

*I ate at McDonald's.*

*I had a Big Mac.*

*I also had a Coke and fries.*

□答對　□答錯

---

\* McDonald's〔mək'dɑnḷdz〕n. 麥當勞

Big Mac〔'bɪɡˏmæk〕n. 麥香堡　　fries〔fraɪz〕n. pl. 薯條

這三句話的意思是「我在麥當勞吃飯。我吃了一個麥香堡。我也喝了可口可樂和吃薯條。」【有關麥當勞的背景說明，請參照「一口氣英語①」7-3】。

如果你吃了中式餐點，你可以說：

I had a pork chop and rice.（我吃了排骨飯。）

I had some vegetables.（我吃了一些蔬菜。）

I also had a bowl of soup.（我也喝了一碗湯。）

【*pork chop* 排骨　rice〔raɪs〕n. 米；飯　bowl〔bol〕n. 碗】

如果你吃牛肉麵，你可以說：

I ate at a noodle shop.（我在麵店吃飯。）

I had beef noodles.（我吃了牛肉麵。）

I also had some side dishes.（我也吃了一些小菜。）

【noodle〔'nudḷ〕n. 麵　*side dish* 小菜】

如果你沒有吃晚餐：

I didn't eat a meal.（我沒有吃飯。）

I skipped dinner.（我不吃晚餐。）

I just had a piece of bread.（我只吃了一片麵包。）

【skip〔skɪp〕v. 跳過；略過　*skip dinner* 不吃晚餐】

問一答三自我測驗

當你背很快變成自覺後，往往會漏掉 a 或 the 等，你自己不覺得，但外國人聽你的英文就不道地了。唯有默寫能注意這些細節。

51. Question: What do you want to do?

Answers: _____

_____

_____

52. Question: May I ask you a question?

Answers: _____

_____

_____

53. Question: What's your favorite fruit?

Answers: _____

_____

_____

54. Question: Did you sleep well?

Answers: _____

_____

_____

55. Question: Can you swim?

Answers: _____

_____

_____

56. Question: How many languages can you speak?

Answers: _____

_____

_____

57. Question: How many are in your class?

Answers: _____

_____

_____

58. Question: Can you play any instruments?

Answers: _____

_____

_____

59. Question: Do you like learning English?

Answers: _____

_____

_____

60. Question: What did you eat last night?

Answers: _____

_____

_____

※ 你寫完後，須訂正答案，將錯誤的地方，用紅筆標出來，
不斷地複習，不斷地唸，你就不會說錯了。

**Question 61**

# *What are you doing tonight?*

（未回答前，勿翻下一頁）

**What are you doing tonight?** 意思是「你今天晚上要做什麼？」源自：What are you planning on doing tonight?（你今天晚上打算做什麼？）可以加長為 What are you doing for fun tonight?（你今天晚上想做什麼好玩的事？）【plan〔plæn〕v. 計劃；打算　*for fun* 爲了樂趣】

下面都是美國人常說的話，意思接近：

**What are you doing tonight?**【第一常用】

What are your plans for tonight?【第四常用】
（你今天晚上有什麼計劃？）

What are you planning for tonight?【第五常用】
（你今天晚上計劃做什麼？）

What's up for tonight?【第三常用】
（你今天晚上要做什麼？）

What's going on tonight?【第二常用】
（你今天晚上計劃做什麼？）

What are you up to tonight?【第六常用】
（你今天晚上想做什麼？）
【*be up to* 著手做】

## Answers 61

*I don't know yet.*

*I'm undecided.*

*I'll probably stay at home.*

□答對　□答錯

　　*I don't know yet.* 的意思是「我還不知道。」可以說成：I'm not sure. ( 我不確定。) *I'm undecided.* ( 我還沒有決定。)【undecided〔͵ʌndɪ'saɪdɪd〕*adj.* 尚未決定的】*I'll probably stay at home.* 意思是「我可能會待在家裡。」也可說成 I might stay at home. ( 我可能會待在家裡。)

如果你打算看電影，就可以說：

　　I'm going to see a movie. ( 我要去看電影。)

　　I plan to see the seven o'clock show.

　　　　( 我打算看七點的電影。)【show〔ʃo〕*n.* 電影】

　　Would you like to join me?

　　　　( 你想和我一起去嗎？)

　　　　【join〔dʒɔɪn〕*v.* 加入；和 ( 某人 ) 一起做同樣的事】

如果你要準備考試，就可以說：

　　I have to study. ( 我必須讀書。)

　　I can't go any place. ( 我哪裡都不能去。)

　　I have a big test tomorrow. ( 我明天有大考。)

**Question 62**

# *How did you get here today?*

（未回答前，勿翻下一頁）

　　美國人爲了避免尷尬，喜歡説：*How did you get here today?* 意思是「你今天怎麼來的？」常簡化爲：How did you get here?（你怎麼來的？）

下面都是美國人常説的話：

*How did you get here today?*【第一常用】

How did you arrive here today?【第五常用】

（你今天怎麼來的？）

I'd like to know how you got here.【第六常用】

（我想知道你怎麼來的。）

Did you take a bus here today?【第四常用】

（你今天搭公車來嗎？）

Did you drive here today?【第二常用】

（你今天開車來嗎？）

Did you get a ride here today?

（今天有人載你來嗎？）【第三常用】

## Answers 62

*I came by bus.*
*I always take the bus.*
*It's cheap and convenient.*

□答對　□答錯

　　*I came by bus.* 意思是「我坐公車來的。」(= *I came here by bus.* ) 也可説成：I got here by bus. ( 我搭公車來的。)

　　*I always take the bus.* 意思是「我總是搭公車。」(= *I always ride the bus.* ) *It's cheap and convenient.* 的意思是「既便宜又方便。」

如果你母親載你來，就可説：

　　　I got a ride here. ( 我坐車來的。)
　　　My mother drove me. ( 我母親開車載我。)
　　　She often drives me around.
　　　( 我去那裡她常常都會開車載我去。)
　　　( = *She takes me everywhere every day.* )

如果你走路來，就可以説：

　　　I walked here. ( 我走路來這裡。)
　　　I don't live far away. ( 我沒有住很遠。)
　　　My home is twenty minutes from here.
　　　( 我家離這裡只要二十分鐘。)

Question 63

# *Who is your best friend?*

（未回答前，勿翻下一頁）

美國大人喜歡問小孩：***Who is your best friend?***（誰是你最好的朋友？）或 Tell me, "Who is your best friend?"（告訴我，「誰是你最好的朋友？」）有時也進一步地問小孩：Tell me about your best friend.（告訴我有關你最好的朋友的事。）

下面是美國人常說的話，我們按照使用頻率排列：

① ***Who is your best friend?***【第一常用】
② Who is your closest friend?【第二常用】
　（誰是你最親密的朋友？）
③ Who is your number one friend?【第三常用】
　（誰是你最好的朋友？）

【close〔klos〕*adj.* 親密的　***number one*** 第一的；最好的】

④ Who's your best pal?
　（誰是你最好的朋友？）
⑤ Who's your best buddy?
　（誰是你最好的朋友？）
⑥ Who do you hang out with?
　（你都跟誰在一起？）

pal〔pæl〕*n.* 夥伴；好友；朋友
buddy〔'bʌdɪ〕*n.* 同伴；夥伴　***hang out with*** 和～在一起

## Answers 63

*My classmate is my best friend.*
*We do everything together.*
*We've known each other for years.*

☐答對 ☐答錯

*My classmate is my best friend.* 的意思是「我的班上同學是我最好的朋友。」可指名道姓地說：My classmate Andy is my best friend. (我的同學安迪是最好的朋友。)【Andy〔'ændɪ〕n. 安迪】
*We do everything together.* 的意思是「我們不管做什麼事都在一起。」*We've known each other for years.* 的意思是「我們已經認識好幾年了。」for years 在此等於 for many years。

如果你最好的朋友是 Pat，你就可以說：

My best friend is named Pat. (我最好的朋友名字叫作派特。)
Pat is my neighbor. (派特是我的鄰居。)
We grew up playing together. (我們從小到大都在一起玩。)
*be named* ～　名字叫作～
neighbor〔'nebɚ〕n. 鄰居　　*grow up*　長大

如果你沒有特別好的朋友，就可說：

I have many good friends. (我有很多好朋友。)
I can't just name one. (我只是沒辦法說出哪個跟我最好。)
I'm lucky because I have quite a few.
(我很幸運，因為我有很多。)
【name〔nem〕v. 說出…的名字　*quite a few*　很多 (= *many*)】

**Question 64**

# *What do you usually eat for lunch?*

（未回答前，勿翻下一頁）

**What do you usually eat for lunch?** 的意思是「你通常午餐吃什麼？」可簡化爲：What do you eat for lunch?（你午餐吃什麼？）

下面都是美國人常説的話，我們按照使用頻率排列：

① ***What do you usually eat for lunch?*** 【第一常用】

② What do you usually have for lunch? 【第二常用】
（你午餐通常吃什麼？）【have〔hæv〕v. 吃】

③ What do you normally eat for lunch? 【第三常用】
（你午餐通常吃什麼？）

④ What do you normally have for lunch?
（你午餐通常吃什麼？）
【normally〔'nɔrml̩ɪ〕adv. 通常】

⑤ What's your typical lunch?
（你午餐通常吃什麼？）

⑥ What's your daily lunch?
（你每天午餐都吃什麼？）
【typical〔'tɪpɪkl̩〕adj. 典型的　daily〔'delɪ〕adj. 每天的】

## Answers 64

*I sometimes have a pork chop.*

*I sometimes have a chicken leg.*

*I'm a meat person.*

□答對 □答錯

*I sometimes have a pork chop.* 的意思是「我有時候吃豬排。」(=*Sometimes I have a pork chop.*)【have = eat pork〔pɔrk〕*n.* 豬肉 chop〔tʃɑp〕*n.* 小肉片 *pork chop* 豬排】*I sometimes have a chicken leg.* 的意思是「我有時候吃雞腿。」(= *Sometimes I have a chicken leg.*)*I'm a meat person.* 的意思是「我很喜歡吃肉。」(=*I like to eat meat.*)也可說成：I'm a meat lover. (我是個愛吃肉的人。)【meat〔mit〕*n.* 肉】

如果你常吃炒飯，就可說：

I usually eat fried rice. (我通常吃炒飯。)

I also have green vegetables. (我也吃綠色蔬菜。)

I sometimes eat bean curd soup. (我有時喝豆腐湯。)

【eat 不可用 drink 代替，中外文化不同，因為湯裡有料，還要用嘴巴嚼。】

fried〔fraɪd〕*adj.* 炒的　　rice〔raɪs〕*n.* 米飯

*bean curd* 豆腐　　soup〔sup〕*n.* 湯

如果你常吃米粉，你就可以說：

I often eat rice noodles. (我常吃米粉。)

I like fried dumplings, too. (我也喜歡鍋貼。)

I also like tomato and egg soup. (我也喜歡蕃茄蛋花湯。)

noodle〔'nudḷ〕*n.* 麵　　*rice noodle* 米粉

dumpling〔'dʌmplɪŋ〕*n.* 水餃　　*fried dumpling* 鍋貼

**Question 65**

# *Do you have any pets?*

（未回答前，勿翻下一頁）

***Do you have any pets?*** 的意思是「你有沒有養任何寵物？」源自：Do you have any kind of pet at home?（你在家有沒有養任何種類的寵物？）【pet〔pɛt〕*n.* 寵物】

下面是美國人常說的話，我們按照使用頻率排列：

① ***Do you have a pet?*** 【第一常用】
② Do you have any pets? 【第二常用】
　　（你有任何寵物嗎？）
③ Do you own any pets? 【第三常用】
　　（你有任何寵物嗎？）【own〔on〕*v.* 擁有】

④ Do you have a pet at home?
　　（你家裡有養寵物嗎？）
⑤ Have you ever had a pet?
　　（你曾經養過寵物嗎？）
⑥ Have you ever owned a pet?
　　（你曾經養過寵物嗎？）【ever〔'ɛvɚ〕*adv.* 曾經】

⑦ Do you have a dog or a cat?
　　（你有養貓或狗嗎？）
⑧ Do you like pets?（你喜歡寵物嗎？）
⑨ Do you like animals?（你喜歡動物嗎？）

**Answers 65**

> *Yes, I do.*
> *My family has a dog.*
> *His name is Lucky.*

□答對　□答錯

　　*Yes, I do.* 在這裡的意思是「是的，我有。」等於 Yes, I have a pet.（是的，我有一隻寵物。）*My family has a dog.* 的意思是「我家養了一隻狗。」（= *My family owns a dog.*）*His name is Lucky.* 的意思是「牠的名字叫 Lucky。」（= *He is named Lucky.*）【*be named* ~　名字叫作~】

如果沒有寵物，就可説：

　　I wish I did.（要是有就好了。）

　　I love animals.（我很喜歡動物。）

　　But I have no pets.（但是我沒有寵物。）

如果你打算養狗，你就可以説：

　　Not yet.（還沒有。）

　　I plan to get a pet.

　　（我打算找一隻寵物。）

　　I will get a dog next year.

　　（明年我將弄一隻狗過來。）

　　【*not yet*　尚未】

## Question 66

# *What type of music do you like?*

（未回答前，勿翻下一頁）

*What type of music do you like?* 的意思是「你喜歡哪一種音樂？」(=*What kind of music do you like?*)也可說成：What type of music do you like best? ( 你最喜歡什麼類型的音樂？)【kind〔kaɪnd〕*n.* 種類　type〔taɪp〕*n.* 類型】

下面是美國人常說的話：

*What type of music do you like?*【第一常用】

What type of music do you prefer?【第四常用】
（你比較喜歡什麼類型的音樂？）

What type of music do you enjoy the most?
（你最喜歡什麼類型的音樂？）【第五常用】
【prefer〔prɪˋfɝ〕*v.* 比較喜歡　enjoy〔ɪnˋdʒɔɪ〕*v.* 喜歡】

What's your favorite type of music?【第二常用】
（你最喜歡的音樂類型是什麼？）

What's your favorite kind of music?【第三常用】
（你最喜歡什麼種類的音樂？）
【favorite〔ˋfevərɪt〕*adj.* 最喜愛的】

**Answers 66**

*I like pop music.*
*I like lively songs.*
*I like music with great beat.*

□ 答對　□ 答錯

　　*I like pop music.* 的意思是「我喜歡流行歌曲。」pop〔pɑp〕是 popular（流行的）的縮寫，pop music 是「流行歌曲」。*I like lively songs.* 的意思是「我喜歡輕快的歌曲。」【lively〔'laɪvlɪ〕*adj.* 活潑的；輕快的】*I like music with great beat.* 的意思是「我喜歡好節奏的音樂。」【great = good　beat〔bit〕*n.* 拍子；節拍】

如果你喜歡老歌，你就可以說：

　　I prefer older music. ( 我比較喜歡較老的音樂。)

　　I like Andy Williams. ( 我喜歡安迪‧威廉斯。)

　　I really like his song "Moonriver."

　　( 我真的很喜歡他的 Moonriver ( 月河 ) 這首歌。)

　　【prefer〔prɪ'fɝ〕*v.* 比較喜歡】

如果你喜歡其他種類的歌，就可以說：

　　I like folk music. ( 我喜歡民歌。)

　　I like rock and roll. ( 我喜歡搖滾樂。)

　　I like all kinds of music. ( 我喜歡所有的音樂。)

　　folk〔fok〕*adj.* 民俗的；民謠的

　　*folk music* 民謠；民歌音樂　　*rock and roll* 搖滾樂

Question 67

# *What's your favorite season?*

（未回答前，勿翻下一頁）

*What's your favorite season?* 的意思是「你最喜愛什麼季節？」源自：What's your favorite season of the year?（一年當中，你最喜愛什麼季節？）【season〔'sizn〕n. 季節】

下面都是美國人常說的話：

*What's your favorite season?*【第一常用】

What season is your favorite?【第二常用】

（你最喜愛什麼季節？）

What season of the year is your favorite?

（你最喜愛一年中的什麼季節？）【第六常用】

【favorite〔'fevərɪt〕adj. 最喜愛的　n. 最喜愛的人或物】

What season do you like best?【第四常用】

（你最喜歡什麼季節？）

【best 在此等於 the best】

Which season do you like the best?【第五常用】

（你最喜歡哪個季節？）

Which season is your favorite?【第三常用】

（你最喜愛哪個季節？）

---

**Answers 67**

*Spring is my favorite*.
*The weather is perfect*.
*Everything looks new*.

□ 答對　□ 答錯

---

　　***Spring is my favorite***. 的意思是「我最喜愛春天。」
( = *Spring is my favorite season*. ) ***The weather is perfect***.
的意思是「那個時候的天氣最好。」( = *The weather is just
right*. )【perfect〔'pɝfɪkt〕*adj.* 完美的　*just right* 剛好】***Everything
looks new***. 的意思是「每樣事物看起來都很新。」可以加強語
氣說成：Everything looks new and clean. (每樣東西都看
起來既新鮮又乾淨。)

如果你喜歡夏天，你就可以說：

　　I like summer the best. (我最喜歡夏天。)
　　I like hot weather. (我喜歡熱的天氣。)
　　I can go hiking or swimming. (我可以去健行或游泳。)
　　【hike〔haɪk〕*v.* 健行】

如果你喜歡秋天，就可說：

　　I like the fall. (我喜歡秋天。)
　　I like the cool weather. (我喜歡涼爽的天氣。)
　　It's a comfortable season. (它是令人舒服的季節。)
　　fall〔fɔl〕*n.* 秋天　　cool〔kul〕*adj.* 涼爽的
　　comfortable〔'kʌmfɚtəbḷ〕*adj.* 舒服的

**Question 68**

# *What's something you hate to do?*

（未回答前，勿翻下一頁）

　　***What's something you hate to do?*** 的意思是「你討厭做什麼事？」hate 的主要意思是「恨」，但在口語中，常作「討厭；不喜歡」解。這句話可加強語氣說成：What is something you really hate to do?（什麼是你真的很不喜歡做的事？）也有美國人說：What's the thing you hate to do most?（你最不喜歡做什麼事？）

下面是美國人常說的話，我們按照使用頻率排列：

① ***What's something you hate to do?***【第一常用】

② What's something you don't like to do?
　（你不喜歡做什麼事？）【第二常用】

③ What's something you dislike doing?
　（你不喜歡做什麼事？）【第三常用】
　【dislike〔dɪs'laɪk〕v. 不喜歡】

④ What don't you like to do?
　（你不喜歡做什麼事？）

⑤ What do you dislike doing?
　（你不喜歡做什麼事？）

## Answers 68

*I hate doing chores.*

*I hate cleaning my room.*

*I especially hate taking out the garbage.*

□答對　□答錯

*I hate doing chores.* 的意思是「我討厭做家事。」【chores ( tʃɔrz ) n. pl. 雜事；家事 ( = housework )】hate 的後面可接動名詞或不定詞，所以可說成：I hate to do chores. 意思相同。*I hate cleaning my room.* 的意思是「我不喜歡打掃房間。」*I especially hate taking out the garbage.* 的意思是「我特別討厭倒垃圾。」【especially ( ə'spɛʃəlɪ ) adv. 尤其；特別是　*take out* 把~拿出去　garbage ('gɑrbɪdʒ ) n. 垃圾】

可以幽默地說：

I hate taking tests. ( 我討厭考試。)

I don't like the pressure. ( 我不喜歡有壓力。)

It upsets me a lot. ( 它使我很煩惱。)

*take a test* 參加考試　pressure ('prɛʃə ) n. 壓力

upset ( ʌp'sɛt ) v. 使煩惱　*a lot* 很；非常

如果你不喜歡等人，就可說：

I hate waiting for people. ( 我討厭等人。)

I don't like to stand around. ( 我不喜歡呆呆地站著。)

I hate to waste time. ( 我不喜歡浪費時間。)

【*stand around* 發呆地站著】

## Question 69

# *For here or to go?*

（未回答前，勿翻下一頁）

在速食餐廳點餐，通常會被問到：*For here or to go?*
意思是「在這裡吃或帶走？」源自：Is your order for here
or to go?（你點的東西要在這裡吃或帶走？）

【order〔ˋɔrdɚ〕*n.*（在餐廳）點的菜　*for here* 內用；在這裡吃
*to go* 外帶；帶走】

下面是美國人常說的話：

For here or to go?

***For here or to go?***【第一常用】

Is that for here or to go?

（那是要在這裡吃或是帶走？）

【第二常用】

For here or take out?【第四常用】

（在這裡吃或帶走？）

Is that for here or to take out?【第五常用】

（那是要在這裡吃或帶走？）

Would you like that for here or to go?【第三常用】

（那個你想在這裡吃還是帶走？）

【*take out* 外帶】

## Answers 69

> *For here, please.*
> *I'd also like a bag.*
> *I might take some to go later.*

□ 答對　　□ 答錯

　　***For here, please.*** 的意思是「我要在這裡吃。」也可說成：
That would be for here. ( 那是要在這裡吃的。) ***I'd also***
***like a bag.*** 的意思是「我也要一個袋子。」【*would like* 想要】
***I might take some to go later.*** ( 我待會也許會帶一些走。)
( = *I may take some to go later.* )【later (ˈletɚ ) *adv.* 待會】

如果你要帶走，你就可以說：

　　To go, please. ( 要外帶。)
　　I'd like it in a bag. ( 我要用袋子裝。)
　　Can you give me extra napkins?
　　( 你能不能多給我一些餐巾紙？)
　　extra (ˈɛkstrə ) *adj.* 額外的【在此等於 more 】
　　napkin (ˈnæpkɪn ) *n.* 餐巾

如果你要兩個袋子，就可說：

　　I want it to go. ( 我要外帶。)
　　Can I have two bags? ( 我能不能要兩個袋子？)
　　Can you separate the drinks and the food?
　　( 你能不能把飲料和食物分開？)
　　【separate (ˈsɛpəˌret ) *v.* 使…分開　　drink ( drɪŋk ) *n.* 飲料】

**Question 70**

# *Have you ever gone camping?*

（未回答前，勿翻下一頁）

　　*Have you ever gone camping?* 的意思是「你曾經露過營嗎？」【camp〔kæmp〕v. 露營】在文法書上常說，表經驗，應該用 have been，不能用 *have gone*。

【比較】*I have gone to America.*【誤】

　　　　I have been to America.（我去過美國。）【正】

　　　　have been 表示經驗，have gone 是表示「去了沒有回來」。人在這裡，不能說「我已經去了美國。」只能說「我去過美國。」

　　但在這裡，go camping 是一個動詞成語，表示「去露營」，當作一個動詞來看待，和前面所說的 have gone 不同。

　　*Have you ever gone camping?* 可以加長為：Have you ever gone camping before?（你以前曾經露過營嗎？）或 Have you ever gone camping overnight before?（你以前曾經露營過夜嗎？）camp 也可單獨使用，可說成：Have you ever been camping?（你曾經露過營嗎？）或 Have you ever camped before?（你以前曾經露過營嗎？）也有美國人說：Do you have any camping experience?（你有沒有任何露營的經驗？）

**Answers 70**

*No, I haven't.*
*I've never done that.*
*I hope to do it someday.*

□答對　□答錯

*No, I haven't.* 的意思是「不，我沒有。」在此等於：No, I haven't gone camping before. ( 不，我以前沒去露過營。)
*I've never done that.* 的意思是「我從沒做過。」在此等於 I've never gone camping. ( 我從未去露過營。) *I hope to do it someday.* 在這裡的意思是「我希望將來有一天能去露營。」可簡單說成：I plan to someday. ( 我計劃將來有一天去。)【someday〔'sʌm,de〕adv. ( 將來的 ) 某一天】

如果你去過一次，就可說：

Just once. ( 只有一次。)
I did it one time. ( 我露過一次營。)
I'd like to try it again. ( 我想再試一次。)
【once〔wʌns〕adv. 一次　time〔taɪm〕n. 次數】

如果你去過很多次，就可說：

Many times. ( 很多次。)
I really enjoy it. ( 我真的很喜歡。)
I often do it. ( 我常常去。)
【enjoy〔ɪn'dʒɔɪ〕v. 喜歡】

## Questions 61~70　問一答三自我測驗 ◀◀

背東西背久了以後，會對細節不注意，跟外國人講話的時候會漏掉 s 或 ing，自己不覺得怎麼樣，可是外國人聽起來就不舒服了。

61. Question：What are you doing tonight?

    Answers：＿＿＿＿＿＿＿＿＿＿＿＿＿＿＿＿＿＿＿＿

    ＿＿＿＿＿＿＿＿＿＿＿＿＿＿＿＿＿＿＿＿＿＿＿

    ＿＿＿＿＿＿＿＿＿＿＿＿＿＿＿＿＿＿＿＿＿＿＿

62. Question：How did you get here today?

    Answers：＿＿＿＿＿＿＿＿＿＿＿＿＿＿＿＿＿＿＿＿

    ＿＿＿＿＿＿＿＿＿＿＿＿＿＿＿＿＿＿＿＿＿＿＿

    ＿＿＿＿＿＿＿＿＿＿＿＿＿＿＿＿＿＿＿＿＿＿＿

63. Question：Who is your best friend?

    Answers：＿＿＿＿＿＿＿＿＿＿＿＿＿＿＿＿＿＿＿＿

    ＿＿＿＿＿＿＿＿＿＿＿＿＿＿＿＿＿＿＿＿＿＿＿

    ＿＿＿＿＿＿＿＿＿＿＿＿＿＿＿＿＿＿＿＿＿＿＿

64. Question：What do you usually eat for lunch?

    Answers：＿＿＿＿＿＿＿＿＿＿＿＿＿＿＿＿＿＿＿＿

    ＿＿＿＿＿＿＿＿＿＿＿＿＿＿＿＿＿＿＿＿＿＿＿

    ＿＿＿＿＿＿＿＿＿＿＿＿＿＿＿＿＿＿＿＿＿＿＿

65. Question：Do you have any pets?

    Answers：＿＿＿＿＿＿＿＿＿＿＿＿＿＿＿＿＿＿＿＿

    ＿＿＿＿＿＿＿＿＿＿＿＿＿＿＿＿＿＿＿＿＿＿＿

    ＿＿＿＿＿＿＿＿＿＿＿＿＿＿＿＿＿＿＿＿＿＿＿

66. Question : What type of music do you like?

　　Answers : _____

　　　　　　　_____

　　　　　　　_____

67. Question : What's your favorite season?

　　Answers : _____

　　　　　　　_____

　　　　　　　_____

68. Question : What's something you hate to do?

　　Answers : _____

　　　　　　　_____

　　　　　　　_____

69. Question : For here or to go?

　　Answers : _____

　　　　　　　_____

　　　　　　　_____

70. Question : Have you ever gone camping?

　　Answers : _____

　　　　　　　_____

　　　　　　　_____

※ 你寫完後，須訂正答案，將錯誤的地方，用紅筆標出來，
　　以後說的時候，你就不會漏掉了。

Question 71

# *When you feel depressed, what do you do?*

（未回答前，勿翻下一頁）

* depressed〔dɪ'prɛst〕*adj.* 沮喪的

**When you feel depressed, what do you do?** 的意思是
「當你覺得沮喪時，你會做什麼？」可加長爲：Whenever you
feel sad or depressed, what do you do?（每當你覺得傷心
或沮喪時，你會做什麼？）句中的 what do you do 也可改成
what will you do，但是沒有 what do you do 來得普遍。

下面是美國人常説的話，我們按照使用頻率排列：

① **When you feel depressed, what do you do?**
【第一常用】
② When you feel sad, what do you do?【第二常用】
（當你覺得傷心時，你會怎麼做？）
③ When you feel blue, what do you do?
（當你覺得憂鬱時，你會怎麼做？）【第三常用】
【blue〔blu〕*adj.* 憂鬱的】

④ What do you do to overcome depression?
（你會怎麼克服沮喪？）
⑤ How do you get over being depressed?
（你會如何克服沮喪？）
overcome〔͵ovə'kʌm〕*v.* 克服
depression〔dɪ'prɛʃən〕*n.* 沮喪　*get over* 克服

## Answers 71

*I go outside for fresh air.*
*I try to get some exercise.*
*I might jog or walk.*

□ 答對　□ 答錯

---

\* fresh〔frɛʃ〕*adj.* 新鮮的　　jog〔dʒɑg〕*v.* 慢跑

這三句話的意思是「我會到外面呼吸一點新鮮空氣。我會試著做些運動。我也許會慢跑或散步。」

**去看電影、吃東西，也是紓解壓力的方法：**

I go see a movie. ( 我會去看電影。)

I eat my favorite food. ( 我會吃我最喜愛的食物。)

That always cheers me up.

( 那樣做總是能使我高興。)

***go see a movie*** 去看電影 ( = *go and see a movie* )

***cheer*** *sb.* ***up*** 使某人高興 ( = *make sb. happy* )

**找好朋友，也是紓解壓力的方法：**

I call my best friend. ( 我會打電話給我最好的朋友。)

We talk about my problem.

( 我們會談論我的問題。)

That always makes me feel better.

( 那樣做總是能讓我覺得比較好。)

## Question 72

# *Where did you get that shirt?*

（未回答前，勿翻下一頁）

　　美國人習慣看到你穿漂亮的襯衫，會問：***Where did you get that shirt?***（你那件襯衫哪裡來的？）get 的意思是「買」（=*buy*）或「得到」（=*acquire*）。如果你看到朋友戴很好的錶，你可以說：Where did you get that watch?（你那支錶從哪裡來的？）如果你看到朋友有個鐲子，你可以說：Where did you get that bracelet?（你那個手鐲哪裡來的？）【bracelet〔'breslɪt〕*n.* 手鐲】上面各句都可簡化爲：Where did you get that?（你那個東西哪裡來的？）

下面都是美國人常説的話，我們按照使用頻率排列：

① Where did you get that?【第一常用】
　　（你那個是哪裡來的？）

② ***Where did you get that shirt?***【第二常用】

③ Where did you buy that?【第三常用】
　　（你那個是哪裡買的？）

④ What store did you get that in?
　　（你那個是在哪家商店買的？）

⑤ Where did you find that?
　　（你那個是在哪裡找到的？）

⑥ How did you get that?（你那個是如何獲得的？）

## Answers 72

*At the mall*.
*I bought it*.
*It was on sale*.

□答對　□答錯

* mall〔mɔl〕*n.* 購物中心（= *shopping center* ）
*on sale* 特價；拍賣

*At the mall*. 的意思是「在購物中心。」源自：I got it at the mall.（我在購物中心買的。）*I bought it*. 的意思是「我買的。」可加強語氣說成：I bought it myself.（我自己買的。）*It was on sale*. 的字面意思是「它在特價。」在這裡引申為「這個錶在特價。」

如果是在小店買的，你就可以說：

I bought it at a small shop.（我在一間小店買的。）
It was half-price.（它是半價。）
It was a bargain.（它很便宜。）
【bargain〔ˋbɑrgɪn〕*n.* 便宜貨；特價品】

如果是你媽媽買給你的，就可以說：

It was a gift.（它是個禮物。）
My mom bought it for me.（我媽媽買給我的。）
She has good taste.（她很有品味。）
【gift〔gɪft〕*n.* 禮物　taste〔test〕*n.* 品味】

**Question 73**

# *Tell me about yourself.*

（未回答前，勿翻下一頁）

口試的時候，往往會問你：*Tell me about yourself.* 意思是「告訴我一些關於你自己的事情。」( = *Tell me some things about yourself.* )

下面都是美國人常說的話：

*Tell me about yourself.* 【第一常用】
Tell me a little bit about yourself. 【第二常用】
（告訴我一點關於你的事。）【*a little bit* 一點】
Tell me what you are like. 【第五常用】
（告訴我你是什麼樣的人。）

Please describe yourself. 【第三常用】
（請描述一下你自己。）
Please describe your personality. 【第四常用】
（請描述一下你的個性。）
describe〔dɪ'skraɪb〕*v.* 描述
personality〔͵pɝsn̩'ælətɪ〕*n.* 個性

What kind of person are you? 【第六常用】
（你是個什麼樣的人？）
What kind of personality do you have? 【第七常用】
（你是哪一種個性？）

---

**Answers 73**

## *I'm an easygoing person.*
## *I don't get too emotional.*
## *I just take things day by day.*

□ 答對　□ 答錯

---

\* easygoing〔'izɪ'goɪŋ〕 *adj.* 脾氣隨和的（ = *calm and relaxed* ）
emotional〔ɪ'moʃənḷ〕 *adj.* 情緒激動的

    ***I'm an easygoing person.*** 的意思是「我是個隨和的人。」也
就是「我很隨和。」( = *I'm easygoing.* ) ***I don't get too emotional.***
的意思是「我不會太激動。」( = *I don't get too excited.* ) ***I just take
things day by day.*** 句中的 take 有 undertake（從事）、accept（接
受），或 do（做）的意思。***day by day*** 的意思是「一天天」等於 day
after day 或 every day。整句的意思是「我只是每天做我該做的事。」
( = *I just do what I have to do every day.* )

說完上面三句後，可再接著說：

I work hard at everything I do.（我做每件事都很努力。）
I always give my best effort.（我總是會盡力。）
I'm serious about my future.（我對我的未來很認真。）

***work hard*** 努力　　effort〔'ɛfət〕 *n.* 努力　　***give one's best effort*** 盡全力
serious〔'sɪrɪəs〕 *adj.* 認真的　　future〔'fjutʃə〕 *n.* 未來

可再接著說：

I have many friends.（我有很多朋友。）
I enjoy being around people.（我喜歡和人們相處。）
Friends are important to me.（朋友對我很重要。）

【enjoy〔ɪn'dʒɔɪ〕 *v.* 喜歡　　around〔ə'raʊnd〕 *prep.* 在…週圍】

**Question 74**

# *Do you belong to any clubs?*

（未回答前，勿翻下一頁）

* ***belong to*** 屬於　　club〔klʌb〕*n.* 俱樂部；社團

***Do you belong to any clubs?*** 的意思是「你屬不屬於任何社團？」可加長爲：Do you belong to any clubs or groups at school?（你在學校裡屬不屬於任何學校或團體？）
【group〔grup〕*n.* 團體；群體】

下面是美國人常說的話：

> ***Do you belong to any clubs?***【第一常用】
> Do you participate in any clubs?【第五常用】
> （你有沒有參加任何社團？）
> Do you take part in any clubs?【第六常用】
> （你有沒有參加任何社團？）
> participate〔pɑr'tɪsə,pet〕*v.* 參加
> ***participate in*** 參加　　***take part in*** 參加
>
> Are you a member of any clubs?【第三常用】
> （你是任何社團的成員嗎？）
> Are you in any clubs?【第二常用】
> （你有參加任何社團嗎？）
> Are you on any teams?【第四常用】
> （你有加入任何隊伍嗎？）
> 【member〔'mɛmbɚ〕*n.* 成員　　team〔tim〕*n.* 隊】

## Answers 74

> *No, I don't.*
> *I'm too busy.*
> *I don't have any free time.*
>
> □ 答對　　□ 答錯

* *free time* 空閒時間

*No, I don't.* 在這裡的意思是「不，我不屬於任何社團。」
( = *No, I don't belong to any clubs.* ) *I'm too busy.* 的意思是
「我太忙了。」可加長為：I'm too busy to belong to any clubs.
(我太忙了，沒辦法參加任何社團。) *I don't have any free time.*
的意思是「我沒有任何空閒時間。」

如果你屬於英語社，你就可以說：

Yes, I do. ( 是的，我有參加社團。)
I'm in the English Club. ( 我參加英語社。)
We meet every week. ( 我們每個禮拜聚會一次。)
【meet〔mit〕*v.* 見面】

如果你參加吉他社，你就可以說：

Yes, I'm a member of the Guitar Club.
( 是的，我是吉他社的成員。)【guitar〔gɪˈtɑr〕*n.* 吉他】
I also belong to the Pop Music Club.
( 我也參加熱門音樂社。)【*pop music* 流行音樂】
I'm going to join the Dancing Club in the future.
( 以後我會加入舞蹈社。)
【join〔dʒɔɪn〕*v.* 加入　*in the future* 未來】

**Question 75**

# *What do you do when you get sick?*

（未回答前，勿翻下一頁）

*What do you do when you get sick?* 的意思是「你生病時會怎麼辦？」( = *What do you do when you are ill?* )
【ill〔ɪl〕*adj.* 生病的】美國人也常說：What do you do when you catch cold? ( 當你感冒時，你會怎麼辦？)
【cold〔kold〕*n.* 感冒　*catch cold* 感冒】

下面是美國人常說的話：

*What do you do when you get sick?* 【第一常用】
What do you do when you are sick?
（你生病時會怎麼辦？）【第二常用】
How do you handle a cold?
（你會如何處理感冒？）【第五常用】
【handle〔'hændḷ〕*v.* 處理】

How do you deal with a cold? 【第六常用】
（你會如何處理感冒？）
When you're sick, what do you do? 【第三常用】
（當你生病時，你會怎麼辦？）
If you get sick, what do you do? 【第四常用】
（如果你生病了，你會怎麼辦？）
【*deal with* 處理】

## Answers 75

*I go see a doctor.*

*I get a checkup.*

*I do what the doctor says.*

□答對　□答錯

* checkup〔'tʃɛkˌʌp〕*n.* 健康檢查

*I go see a doctor.* 的意思是「我會去看醫生。」(*= I go to see a doctor.* ) *I get a checkup.* ( 我會做健康檢查。) *I do what the doctor says.* 的意思是「我會照著醫生的話去做。」

如果你會去藥局買藥，就說：

I go to a pharmacy. ( 我會到藥局去。)
I buy some medicine. ( 我會買一些藥。)
I follow the instructions carefully.
( 我會謹慎地按照說明服藥。)

pharmacy〔'fɑrməsɪ〕*n.* 藥局　　follow〔'fɑlo〕*v.* 遵照
instructions〔ɪn'strʌkʃənz〕*n. pl.* 指示；說明

休息和睡覺是治病最好的方法：

I just stay in bed. ( 我只是待在床上。)
I sleep as much as I can. ( 我儘可能多睡覺。)
I get lots of rest. ( 我會充份休息。)

*as…as one can* 儘可能…　　*lots of* 很多；大量的
rest〔rɛst〕*n.* 休息

┌─ **Question 76** ─────────────────────────────

# *Which country would you like to visit?*

（未回答前，勿翻下一頁）

└──────────────────────────────────────

\* visit〔'vɪzɪt〕v. 拜訪；參觀；遊覽

**Which country would you like to visit?** 的意思是「你想要去哪一個國家玩？」可以加強語氣說成：Which country would you most like to visit?（你最想要去哪一個國家玩？）(= *Which country would you like to visit the most?*)

下面都是美國人常說的話：

**Which country would you like to visit?** 【第一常用】
What country do you want to visit?【第三常用】
（你想去哪個國家玩？）

Where would you like to visit?【第二常用】
（你想去哪裡玩？）
Where do you want to go to the most?【第四常用】
（你最想去哪裡？）

Which country would you choose to visit if you could?
（如果可以的話，你會選擇去哪一個國家？）【第五常用】
If you could, where would you most like to visit?
（如果可以的話，你最想去哪裡玩？）【第六常用】
【choose〔tʃuz〕v. 選擇】

**Answers 76**

*I'd like to visit the States.*

*I want to go to San Francisco.*

*I hope to see the Golden Gate Bridge.*

□答對 □答錯

   *I'd like to visit the States.* 的意思是「我想要去美國玩。」
the States (美國) 也可說成 the U.S.、the U.S.A.，或
America。*I want to go to San Francisco.* 的意思是「我想
去舊金山。」*I hope to see the Golden Gate Bridge.* 的意思是
「我想去看金門大橋。」【San Francisco〔ˌsænfrənˈsɪsko〕*n.* 舊金山
*Golden Gate Bridge* 金門大橋】

如果你想去希臘，就可說：

   I want to visit Greece. (我想去希臘玩。)

   I hear it's really beautiful.

      (我聽說希臘很漂亮。)

   I also love historical places. (我也喜歡古蹟。)

   Greece〔gris〕*n.* 希臘    hear〔hɪr〕*v.* 聽說

   historical〔hɪsˈtɔrɪkḷ〕*adj.* 歷史的    *historical place* 古蹟

如果你想去歐洲，你就可以說：

   I want to visit Europe. (我想去歐洲玩。)

   I want to see many countries. (我想去很多國家看看。)

   I guess England would be my first choice.

      (我想英國會是我的第一個選擇。)

   【Europe〔ˈjʊrəp〕*n.* 歐洲    guess〔gɛs〕*v.* 猜想；認為】

Question 77

# *What time do you get up?*

（未回答前，勿翻下一頁）

*What time do you get up?* 的意思是「你幾點起床？」可加長爲：What time do you usually get up in the morning?（你早上通常幾點起床？）【*get up* 起床】

下面是美國人常說的話，我們按照使用頻率排列：

① *What time do you get up?*【第一常用】

② What time do you wake up?【第二常用】
   （你幾點起床？）

③ What time do you get out of bed?【第三常用】
   （你何時起床？）

   【*wake up* 醒來　*get out of bed* 起床】

④ What time do you rise and shine?【第四常用】
   （你何時起床？）

⑤ What time do you roll out of bed in the morning?
   （你早上什麼時候滾下床？）【第五常用】

   *rise and shine* 快起床
   *roll out of bed* 起床（= *roll out*）

上面各句的 What time 均可改爲 When，使用頻率不變。最後兩句是幽默用語。

## Answers 77

*I get up at six a.m.*

*On weekdays it's always at six.*

*On weekends I sleep in.*

□答對　□答錯

---

\* ***a.m.*** 早上　　weekday〔'wik‚de〕*n.* 平日

***sleep in*** 晚起床（= *sleep late*）

***I get up at six a.m.*** 的意思是「我早上六點起床。」可簡化
為：I get up at six.（我六點起床。）***On weekdays it's always
at six.*** 的意思是「平日總是六點鐘起床。」***On weekends I sleep
in.*** 的意思是「在週末，我會晚起。」

也可以幽默地這樣回答：

I wake up at six-thirty.（我在六點半起床。）

My alarm wakes me up.（我的鬧鐘會把我叫醒。）

I hate getting up so early.（我討厭這麼早起床。）

alarm〔ə'lɑrm〕*n.* 鬧鐘（= *alarm clock*）

hate〔het〕*v.* 討厭；不喜歡

如果你通常很早起床，就可說：

I'm up at five-thirty.（我五點半起床。）

I get up earlier than most.（我比大多數人早起。）

I usually jog or do some exercise.

（我通常會慢跑或做一些運動。）

most〔most〕*n.* 大多數人（= *most people*）

jog〔dʒɑg〕*v.* 慢跑　　exercise〔'ɛksɚ‚saɪz〕*n.* 運動

Question 78

# *Can you cook?*

（未回答前，勿翻下一頁）

*Can you cook?* 的意思是「你
會不會煮飯？」可加強語氣説成：
Can you cook very well? ( 你是
不是很會煮飯？ ) 或 Can you
cook many dishes? ( 你會不會做
很多菜？ )【dish〔dɪʃ〕*n.* 菜餚】

Can you cook?

下面都是美國人常説的話：

*Can you cook?*【第一常用】

Are you a good cook?【第三常用】
（你很會煮飯嗎？）

Do you know how to cook?【第二常用】
（你知道如何煮飯嗎？）
【cook〔kʊk〕*v.* 煮飯；作菜　*n.* 廚師】

Do you cook a lot?【第六常用】
（你常煮飯嗎？ )【*a lot* 常常】

Do you like to cook?【第四常用】
（你喜歡煮飯嗎？）

Do you like cooking?【第五常用】
（你喜歡煮飯嗎？）

## Answers 78

> ### *Sure, I can.*
> ### *But I'm not a good cook.*
> ### *I can cook some simple dishes.*

□ 答對　　□ 答錯

* simple〔ˋsɪmpḷ〕*adj.* 簡單的

　　***Sure, I can.*** 的意思是「當然，我會。」( = *Sure, I can cook.* )
句中的 Sure 可改成 Yes。***But I'm not a good cook.*** 的意思
是「但是我不太會煮飯。」( = *But I don't cook very well.* ) But
是轉承語，連接前面句子。***I can cook some simple dishes.*** 的
意思是「我會煮幾道簡單的菜。」

如果你很會煮飯，你就可以說：

　　Yes, I can. ( 是的，我會。)
　　I enjoy cooking a lot. ( 我很喜歡煮飯。)
　　I can cook many Chinese dishes.
　　( 我會煮很多中國菜。)
　　【enjoy〔ɪnˋdʒɔɪ〕*v.* 喜歡　　*a lot* 非常】

如果你完全不會煮飯，你就可以說：

　　Not at all. ( 一點也不會。)
　　I'm terrible in the kitchen.
　　( 我很不會煮飯。) ( = *I'm a really bad cook.* )
　　Cooking food is something I try to avoid.
　　( 我會儘量避免煮飯。)
　　***not at all*** 一點也不　　terrible〔ˋtɛrəbḷ〕*adj.* 糟糕的
　　avoid〔əˋvɔɪd〕*v.* 避免

## Question 79

# *Do you have a nickname?*

（未回答前，勿翻下一頁）

*Do you have a nickname?* 的意思是「你有沒有綽號？」

【nickname（ˊnɪkˌnem）*n.* 綽號；暱稱】美國社會和中國社會一樣，常會取一個綽號，來代替真正的名字，以表示親密。

下面是美國人常說的話，我們按照使用頻率排列：

① *Do you have a nickname?*【第一常用】

② Do you have any nicknames?

（你有任何綽號嗎？）【第二常用】

③ Do you have any special names that friends call you?【第三常用】

（你有任何朋友用來叫你的特殊名字嗎？）

④ What do your friends call you?

（你的朋友怎麼稱呼你？）

⑤ What do your parents call you?

（你的父母怎麼叫你？）

⑥ Do your friends have a nickname for you?

（你的朋友有幫你取綽號嗎？）

## Answers 79

*No, I don't.*
*I don't have any nicknames.*
*Everyone just calls me by my name.*

□答對　□答錯

*No, I don't.* 在這裡的意思是「不，我沒有。」(= *No, I don't have a nickname.* ) *I don't have any nicknames.* 的意思是「我沒有任何綽號。」*Everyone just calls me by my name.* 的意思是「大家只是叫我的名字。」【by 在此作「按照」解，等於 according to】

如果你有英文小名，就可以說：

Yes, I have an English nickname.
（有，我有英文暱稱。）
My English name is Jennifer.
（我的英文名字是珍妮佛。）
People call me Jenny. ( 大家都叫我珍妮。)
【Jennifer (ˈdʒɛnɪfə ) n. 珍妮佛　Jenny (ˈdʒɛnɪ ) n. 珍妮】

如果你的英文名字是 David（大衛），你的暱稱可能是 Dave 或 Davey：

Yes, I have a nickname. ( 有，我有一個暱稱。)
My parents call me Dave. ( 我的父母叫我戴夫。)
My friends call me Davey. ( 我的朋友叫我戴維。)
【Dave〔dev〕n. 戴夫　Davey (ˈdevɪ ) n. 戴維】

Question 80

# *How do you celebrate your birthday?*

（未回答前，勿翻下一頁）

\* celebrate〔'sɛlə,bret〕v. 慶祝

    *How do you celebrate your birthday?* 的意思是「你如何慶祝你的生日？」可能源自：How do you usually celebrate your birthday?（你通常如何慶祝你的生日？）或 How do you celebrate your birthday every year?（你每年如何慶祝你的生日？）

下面是美國人常說的話：

    *How do you celebrate your birthday?*【第一常用】
On your birthday, how do you celebrate?
（在你生日那天，你會怎麼慶祝？）【第二常用】
What do you do to celebrate your birthday?
（你會怎麼慶祝你的生日？）【第三常用】

In what ways do you like to celebrate your
   birthday?（你喜歡怎麼慶祝你的生日？）【第六常用】
What do you do for fun on your birthday?
（你生日時你會做什麼好玩的事？）【第四常用】
Do you celebrate your birthday in any special way?
（你會用什麼特別的方式來慶祝生日嗎？）【第五常用】
【way〔we〕n. 方式　*for fun* 為了樂趣】

## Answers 80

*My family buys a cake.*

*We eat a nice meal together.*

*Everyone sings "Happy Birthday" to me.*

□ 答對　□ 答錯

* meal〔mil〕*n.* 一餐

　　*My family buys a cake.* 的意思是「我的家人會買一個蛋糕。」(= *Someone in my family buys a cake.*) *We eat a nice meal together.* (我們會一起吃一頓大餐。) *Everyone sings "Happy Birthday" to me.* 的意思是「大家會對我唱『生日快樂歌』。」

如果和朋友一起慶祝，就可說：

I celebrate with a party. (我會開派對慶祝。)

My family and friends all get together.

　(我的家人和朋友都會聚在一起。)

They give me gifts and cards. (他們會送我禮物和卡片。)

【*get together* 聚在一起　gift〔gɪft〕*n.* 禮物】

如果你不慶祝生日，你就說：

I don't celebrate on my birthday. (我不會慶祝生日。)

It's just another day. (那只是個普通的日子。)

My family never celebrate birthdays.

　(我們家從不慶祝生日。)

## Questions 71~80　問一答三自我測驗

背書背一段時間後，一定要默寫，否則你就會不小心漏掉一些字，像 s，ed，a 等，會讓外國人聽起來覺得不舒服。默寫可加深印象。

71. Question：When you feel depressed, what do you do?

　　Answers：_____

　　　　　　_____

　　　　　　_____

72. Question：Where did you get that shirt?

　　Answers：_____

　　　　　　_____

　　　　　　_____

73. Question：Tell me about yourself.

　　Answers：_____

　　　　　　_____

　　　　　　_____

74. Question：Do you belong to any clubs?

　　Answers：_____

　　　　　　_____

　　　　　　_____

75. Question：What do you do when you get sick?

　　Answers：_____

　　　　　　_____

　　　　　　_____

76. Question : Which country would you like to visit?

Answers : _____

_____

_____

77. Question : What time do you get up?

Answers : _____

_____

_____

78. Question : Can you cook?

Answers : _____

_____

_____

79. Question : Do you have a nickname?

Answers : _____

_____

_____

80. Question : How do you celebrate your birthday?

Answers : _____

_____

_____

※ 你寫完後，須訂正答案，將錯誤的地方，用紅筆標出來，
以後說的時候，你就不會漏掉了。

**Question 81**

# *What's your ideal job?*

（未回答前，勿翻下一頁）

\* ideal〔aɪˈdiəl〕*adj.* 理想的

**What's your ideal job?** 的意思是「你理想的工作是什麼？」也可說成：In your mind, what's the perfect job for you?（在你的心目中，什麼是最好的工作？）
【perfect〔ˈpɝfɪkt〕*adj.* 完美的】

下面是美國人常說的話，我們按照使用頻率排列：

① **What's your ideal job?**【第一常用】
② What's your dream job?【第二常用】
　（你理想的工作是什麼？）
③ What would be the perfect job for you?
　（你理想的工作是什麼？）【第三常用】
　【dream〔drim〕*adj.* 理想的；夢想的】

④ What kind of job would you love to have?
　（你很想擁有哪一種工作？）
⑤ What type of job do you most desire?
　（你最想要哪一種工作？）

　kind〔kaɪnd〕*n.* 種類　　*love to V.* 很喜歡…
　type〔taɪp〕*n.* 類型　　desire〔dɪˈzaɪr〕*v.* 想要

## Answers 81

*I'd like to own a company.*

*I want to be my own boss.*

*I'd like to control my destiny.*

□ 答對　□ 答錯

* destiny〔ˋdɛstənɪ〕*n.* 命運　　boss〔bɔs〕*n.* 老板

*I'd like to own a company.* 的意思是「我想要擁有一間公司。」也可說成：I'd like to have my own business.（我想要有自己的事業。）*I want to be my own boss.* 的意思是「我想自己當老板。」(＝ *I want to be a boss.*）*I'd like to control my destiny.* 的意思是「我想要控制自己的命運。」也可說成：I want to determine my future.（我想決定自己的未來。）

【determine〔dɪˋtɝmɪn〕*v.* 決定】

如果你想教書，就可以說：

I want to be a professor.（我想當教授。）

I'd love to teach English.（我很想教英文。）

I'd be the best university teacher.

（我會是最好的大學老師。）【用 I'd 比 I'll 謙虛】

【professor〔prəˋfɛsɚ〕*n.* 教授　　university〔͵junəˋvɝsətɪ〕*n.* 大學】

如果你想當醫生，就可說：

I want to be a doctor.（我想當醫生。）

I'd like to cure diseases.（我想要治病。）

I want to help people in need.（我想幫助需要幫助的人。）

cure〔kjur〕*v.* 治療　　disease〔dɪˋziz〕*n.* 疾病

*in need* 需要中的；貧困中的

**Question 82**

# *Who is the person you admire most?*

（未回答前，勿翻下一頁）

* admire〔əd'maɪr〕v. 欽佩；讚賞

**Who is the person you admire most?** 的意思是「你最敬佩誰？」可以加長爲：In the world today, who is the person you admire most? (在現今的世界上，你最敬佩誰？) 或 From history, who is the personyou admire most? (在歷史上，你最敬佩誰？)【history〔'hɪstrɪ〕n. 歷史】

下面都是美國人常説的話，我們按照使用頻率排列：

① **Who is the person you admire most?**【第一常用】

② Who do you admire the most?【第二常用】
 （你最欽佩的人是誰？）

③ Who is someone you really admire?【第三常用】
 （你眞的很欽佩的人是誰？）

④ Who is someone you look up to?
 （你尊敬的人是誰？）

⑤ Who is someone you really respect a lot?
 （你眞的非常尊敬的人是誰？）

⑥ Who is someone you think highly of?
 （你尊敬的人是誰？）

> ***look up to*** 尊敬　 respect〔rɪ'spɛkt〕v. 尊敬
> ***a lot*** 非常　 ***think highly of*** 尊敬；重視

## Answers 82

> ### *I admire my father most.*
> ### *He's my hero.*
> ### *He's the greatest man I know.*

□答對　□答錯

---

\* hero〔ˈhɪro〕*n.* 英雄　　great〔gret〕*adj.* 偉大的

**I admire my father most.** 的意思是「我最欽佩我爸爸。」
(=*I admire my father the most.* )【沒有比較對象時，most =
the most】**He's my hero.** 的意思是「他是我心目中的英雄。」
(=*He's a hero in my mind.* ) **He's the greatest man I know.**
的意思是「他是我所知道最偉大的人。」

如果你欽佩你母親，就可說：

I respect my mother most. ( 我最尊敬我母親。)
She works harder than anyone. ( 她比任何人都努力。)
She sacrifices a lot for me. ( 她爲我犧牲很多。)
　【*work hard* 努力　　sacrifice〔ˈsækrə,faɪs〕*v.* 犧牲】

如果你喜歡你的老師，就可說：

I admire one of my teachers. ( 我最欽佩我的一位老師。)
She's an excellent educator. ( 她是個很優秀的教育家。)
I want to be as smart as her. ( 我想要跟她一樣聰明。)
　【文法上，her 應說成 she，但是美國人習慣用 her。】
excellent〔ˈɛksḷənt〕*adj.* 極佳的；優秀的
educator〔ˈɛdʒʊ,ketɚ〕*n.* 教育家　　smart〔smɑrt〕*adj.* 聰明的

## Question 83

# *Are you nearsighted?*

（未回答前，勿翻下一頁）

\* nearsighted（'nɪr'saɪtɪd）*adj.* 近視的

***Are you nearsighted?*** 的意思是「你有沒有近視？」
可加長爲：Are you nearsighted or farsighted?（你有沒
有近視或遠視？）【farsighted（'far'saɪtɪd）*adj.* 遠視的】可以客
氣地問：May I ask, "Are you nearsighted?"（可不可以
請問：「你有沒有近視？」）

下面都是美國人常說的話，我們按照使用頻率排列：

① ***Are you nearsighted?***【第一常用】

② Are your eyes nearsighted?【第二常用】
（你的眼睛有近視嗎？）

③ How is your vision?【第三常用】
（你的視力如何？）

④ How is your eyesight?（你的視力如何？）
【vision（'vɪʒən）*n.* 視力　eyesight（'aɪ,saɪt）*n.* 視力】

⑤ Do you have good eyesight?
（你的視力好嗎？）

⑥ Do you have 20/20 vision?
（你兩隻眼睛都有 2.0 的視力嗎？）

## Answers 83

### *I'm nearsighted.*
### *Everyone in my family is.*
### *We all have bad eyesight.*

□ 答對　　□ 答錯

\* eyesight〔'aɪˌsaɪt〕*n.* 視力

　　*I'm nearsighted.* 的意思是「我近視。」可接著説：I can't see things far away. ( 遠的東西我看不到。)【*far away* 遠處的】*Everyone in my family is.* 在這裡的意思是「我的家人都近視。」( = *Everyone in my family is nearsighted.* ) *We all have bad eyesight.* 的意思是「我們的視力都不好。」為了避免別人對你有壞的印象，可接著説：With glasses I can see perfectly fine. ( 戴了眼鏡，我就可以看得很清楚。)【glasses〔'glæsɪz〕*n. pl.* 眼鏡　　perfectly〔'pɝfɪktlɪ〕*adv.* 完全地　　fine〔faɪn〕*adv.* 很好地】

視力不好，也可以這樣説：

　　I have bad eyesight. ( 我的視力不好。)
　　I have awful vision. ( 我的視力很差。)
　　I'm as blind as a bat. ( 我的視力很差。)
　　awful〔'ɔful〕*adj.* 糟糕的　　blind〔blaɪnd〕*adj.* 瞎的
　　bat〔bæt〕*n.* 蝙蝠　　*as blind as a bat* 近乎全瞎；視力很差

如果你視力很好，就可以説：

　　I'm not. ( 我沒有。)
　　I have good vision. ( 我的視力很好。)
　　My eyes are pretty good. ( 我的視力相當好。)
　　vision〔'vɪʒən〕*n.* 視力　　eyes〔aɪz〕*n. pl.* 視力
　　pretty〔'prɪtɪ〕*adv.* 相當

**Question 84**

# *Do you like to read?*

（未回答前，勿翻下一頁）

    ***Do you like to read?*** 的意思是「你喜不喜歡看書？」可加強語氣說成：Do you like to read a lot?（你是不是很喜歡看書？）【*a lot* 非常（＝*very much*）】可接著問：What do you like to read?（你喜歡看什麼書？）或 What kind of books do you like to read?（你喜歡看哪一類的書？）

下面都是美國人常說的話：

***Do you like to read?***【第一常用】
Do you read a lot?（你常看書嗎？）【第三常用】
Do you read much?（你常看書嗎？）【第四常用】
 【*a lot* 常常】

Do you enjoy reading?（你喜歡看書嗎？）【第二常用】
Are you a big reader?【第七常用】
（你是不是個很愛看書的人？）
Are you an avid reader?【第八常用】
（你是不是個很愛看書的人？）【avid（ˋævɪd）*adj.* 熱愛的】

Do you do a lot of reading?【第五常用】
（你看很多書嗎？）
Do you do much reading?【第六常用】
（你看很多書嗎？）

---

### Answers 84

*I love to read.*

*I read the newspaper every day.*

*I try to read as much as I can.*

□ 答對　□ 答錯

---

\* *as…as one can* 儘可能…

*I love to read.* 的意思是「我非常喜歡看書。」( = *I like to read very much.* ) *I read the newspaper every day.* 的意思是「我每天看報紙。」newspaper〔'njuz,pepɚ〕可簡化成 paper，意思都是「報紙」。*I try to read as much as I can.* ( 我儘可能多閱讀。)

如果你喜歡看英文小說，就可說：

I really enjoy reading. ( 我很喜歡閱讀。)

【really 在此作「很」解】

I like English novels. ( 我喜歡英文小說。)

It's a great way to learn English.

( 它是學英文很好的方法。)

【novel〔'nɑvl〕*n.* 小說　great〔gret〕*adj.* 很棒的】

如果你不常閱讀，可幽默地回答說：

I sure do. ( 我當然喜歡。)

I wish I could read a few hours a day.

( 要是我一天能讀幾個小時就好了。)

Regrettably, I'm just too busy. ( 遺憾的是，我就是太忙了。)

sure〔ʃur〕*adv.* 當然

regrettably〔rɪ'grɛtəblɪ〕*adv.* 令人遺憾的是 ( = *regretfully* )

**Question 85**

# *How much TV do you watch?*

（未回答前，勿翻下一頁）

　　*How much TV do you watch?* 的意思是「你看多少電視？」(= *How much time do you spend watching TV?*) 可更明白地說：How much TV do you watch every day? ( 你每天看多少電視？) 如果問「你的電視多少錢買的？」應該說：How much was your TV? 或 How much did your TV cost?

　　下面是美國人常說的話，我們按照使用頻率排列，第一、二句使用頻率接近：

① *How much TV do you watch?*【第一常用】

② Do you watch a lot of TV?【第二常用】
　　( 你是不是看很多電視？)

③ Do you watch much TV?【第三常用】
　　( 你是不是看很多電視？)

④ Do you spend a lot of time watching TV?
　　( 你是不是花很多時間看電視？)

⑤ Do you spend much time watching TV?
　　( 你是不是花很多時間看電視？)

⑥ How many hours of TV do you watch every
　　day? ( 你每天看幾個小時的電視？)

---

**Answers 85**

> *I watch a lot.*
> *On weekdays, several hours.*
> *On weekends, half the day.*
>
> □答對　□答錯

---

\* weekday〔'wik,de〕*n.* 平日　　weekend〔'wik'ɛnd〕*n.* 週末

　　*I watch a lot.* 的意思是「我看很多。」在此引申爲「我看很多電視。」(= *I watch a lot of TV.*) *On weekdays, several hours.* (在週一至週五,看幾個小時。)(= *Every weekday, I watch several hours of TV.*) *On weekends, half the day.* 字面的意思是「在週末,半天。」在這裡引申爲「在週末,看半天的電視。」(= *On weekends, I watch TV half the day.*)
half the day 字面意思是「半天」,是指「半個白天」,也就是 all afternoon (整個下午) 或 all evening (整個晚上)。

很少看電視,就可以說:

> I seldom watch television. (我很少看電視。)
> I prefer other things instead.
> (我反而比較喜歡其他事物。)
> I enjoy surfing the Net. (我喜歡上網。)

seldom〔'sɛldəm〕*adv.* 很少　　prefer〔prɪ'fɝ〕*v.* 比較喜歡
instead〔ɪn'stɛd〕*adv.* 作爲代替;取而代之
enjoy〔ɪn'dʒɔɪ〕*v.* 喜歡　　surf〔sɝf〕*v.* 衝浪
Net〔nɛt〕*n.* 網際網路　　*surf the Net* 瀏覽網際網路

## Question 86

# *How do I get to your home?*

（未回答前，勿翻下一頁）

　　*How do I get to your home?* 的意思是「我要如何才能到你家？」可客氣地說：Please tell me, "How do I get to your home?"（請告訴我：「我要如何才能到你家？」）your home 美國人也常說成 your place 或 your house，成為：How do I get to your place?（= *How do I get to your house?*）意思相同。

下面都是美國人常說的話：

**How do I get to your home?**【第一常用】
Please give me directions to your home.
（請告訴我你家怎麼走。）【第四常用】
Can you give me directions to your home?
（你可不可以告訴我你家怎麼走？）【第三常用】
【directions〔dəˋrɛkʃənz〕*n. pl.*（行路的）指引】

What should I do to get to your home?【第五常用】
（要去你家我該怎麼做？）
How should I go to get to your home?【第六常用】
（我該怎麼走才能去你家？）
What are the directions to your home?【第二常用】
（你家該怎麼走？）
【*get to* 到達】

## Answers 86

*I live in Mu Cha.*
*Take the MRT to the zoo.*
*My home is five minutes away.*

□答對　□答錯

* ***MRT*** 捷運（= *Mass Rapid Transit*）
　 away〔ə'we〕*adv.* (脫離；移動) 向那邊

　　*I live in Mu Cha.* 的意思是「我住在木柵。」***Take the MRT to the zoo.*** 的意思是「坐捷運到動物園。」***My home is five minutes away.*** 的意思是「我家距那裡五分鐘。」(= *My home is five minutes away from there.*)【*away from there* 離那裡】

如果你住在世貿附近，你就可以説：

　　My home is on Keelung Road. ( 我家在基隆路。)
　　It's not far from the World Trade Center.
　　( 離世貿不遠。)
　　Take a bus or the MRT. ( 要搭公車或捷運。)
　　【trade〔tred〕*n.* 貿易　　***World Trade Center*** 世界貿易中心】

如果你住在天母，你就可以説：

　　My home is in Tien Mu. ( 我家在天母。)
　　I live near the American School.
　　( 我住在美國學校附近。)
　　Many buses go by there. ( 有很多公車經過那裡。)
　　【***go by*** 經過】

## Question 87

# *Where's the nearest ATM?*

（未回答前，勿翻下一頁）

　　*Where's the nearest ATM?* 的意思是「最近的提款機在哪裡？」【*ATM* 自動提款機（＝*automatic-teller machine*）】 ATM 也可說成：cash machine 或 bank machine，詳見「一口氣英語⑦」p.2-8。這句話源自：Where's the nearest ATM from here?（距離這裡最近的提款機在哪裡？）可以禮貌地說：Can you tell me where there is an ATM?（能不能告訴我哪裡有提款機？）句中的 where there is an ATM 是名詞子句，做 tell 的直接受詞。

下面是美國人常說的話：

*Where's the nearest ATM?*【第一常用】
Is there an ATM nearby?【第二常用】
（附近有提款機嗎？）
Is there a bank machine nearby?【第三常用】
（附近有提款機嗎？）【nearby（ˈnɪrˈbaɪ）*adv.* 在附近】

Do you know if there's an ATM in this area?
（你知道這個地區有沒有提款機？）【第五常用】
Do you know where the nearest ATM is?【第六常用】
（你知道最近的提款機在哪裡嗎？）
I'm looking for an ATM.【第四常用】
（我在找提款機。）【*look for* 尋找】

## Answers 87

*There's one on this street.*
*It's one block that way.*
*You'll see it on your right.*

□ 答對　□ 答錯

* block〔blɑk〕*n.* 街區
　right〔raɪt〕*n.* 右邊　*adj.* 右邊的

　*There's one on this street.* 的意思是「在這條街上就有一台。」
也可說成：There's one around here. ( 在這附近就有一台。)
*It's one block that way.* ( 就在那邊，過一個路口。) one block
在這裡是指「過一個路口」，一條街往往有好幾個路口。*You'll*
*see it on your right.* ( 你會看到它就在你的右手邊。) ( = *You'll*
*see it on your right side.* )

如果在附近有銀行，就可以說：
　There's a bank around the corner. ( 在轉角有家銀行。)
　【corner〔ˈkɔrnɚ〕*n.* 轉角】
　They have a 24-hour machine. ( 他們有二十四小時的機器。)
　Just take a left up ahead. ( 只要向前走，左轉。)

　left〔lɛft〕*n.* 左邊　*take a left* 左轉
　up 在此作「沿…走過去」*up ahead* 在此是指「往前走過去」，是 up
　the street ahead of you ( 沿著前面這條街走過去 ) 的省略。

如果你不知道，就可以說：
　I'm sorry. ( 很抱歉。)
　I don't know. ( 我不知道。)
　I've no idea. ( 我不知道。)

## Question 88

# *What's tomorrow's forecast?*

（未回答前，勿翻下一頁）

*What's tomorrow's forecast?* 的字面意思是「明天的天氣預報是什麼？」【forecast〔'for͵kæst〕n. 預測；天氣預報】也就是我們平常所說的「天氣預報說，明天天氣怎樣？」。

【比較】下面兩句話意思相同，都常說：

> *What's tomorrow's forecast?*【城市人喜歡說】
> What's tomorrow's weather?【鄉下人常說】
> （明天的天氣怎麼樣？）

*What's tomorrow's forecast?* 源自 What's tomorrow's weather forecast? 可以加長為 Do you know what tomorrow's weather forecast is?（你知不知道，明天的天氣預報怎樣？）( = *Do you know "What is tomorrow's weather report"?* ) 也有美國人常說：What's the weather forecast for tomorrow?（明天的天氣預報怎樣？）( = *What's the weather report for tomorrow?* ) 或 What's tomorrow going to be like?（明天天氣會怎樣？）( = *What's tomorrow's weather going to be like?* )

美國人聚會，為了避免尷尬，沒有話說，通常會談論天氣，如果今天天氣不好，他們會說：Today's weather is awful. Is tomorrow going to be nice?（今天天氣很糟糕。是不是明天天氣會變好呢？）

---

**Answers 88**

# I'm not sure.
# I haven't heard.
# I have no idea.

□ 答對　□ 答錯

---

***I'm not sure.*** 的意思是「我不確定。」(=*I'm not sure what tomorrow's forecast is.*) ***I haven't heard.*** 的意思是「我沒有聽說。」可以加強語氣說成：I haven't heard yet. (我還沒有聽說。) ***I have no idea.*** 的意思是「我不知道。」可以加強語氣說成：I have no idea at all. (我一點都不知道。) 或 I have absolutely no idea. (我完全不知道。)【absolutely〔'æbsə,lutlɪ〕*adv.* 完全地；絕對地】

如果明天天氣好，就可以說：

　　It's going to be nice. (天氣會很好。)

　　The forecast is for sunny skies.

　　　(天氣預報說會陽光普照。)【skies〔skaɪz〕*n. pl.* 氣候】

　　It's supposed to be clear all day. (明天整天應該都很晴朗。)

　　【*be supposed to* 應該　　clear〔klɪr〕*adj.* 晴朗的】

　　第二句為什麼用 for 呢？所有字典都查不到，但美國人常說，應該把它當作慣用句來背。

天氣不好的話，就可以說：

　　The forecast is bad. (天氣預報很糟糕。)

　　It's going to rain all day. (會下一整天的雨。)

　　The temperature is going to drop. (氣溫會下降。)

　　【temperature〔'tɛmpərətʃə〕*n.* 溫度　　drop〔drɑp〕*v.* (溫度) 下降】

**Question 89**

# What's your happiest memory?

（未回答前，勿翻下一頁）

\* memory〔'mɛmərɪ〕*n.* 記憶；回憶

外國人在聊天的時候，常會問到：
***What's your happiest memory?***（你
最快樂的回憶是什麼？）或 What's
your happiest childhood memory?
（你童年時期最快樂的回憶是什麼？）
【childhood〔'tʃaɪld,hʊd〕*n.* 童年】

**What's your happiest memory?**

下面是美國人常說的話：

***What's your happiest memory?***【第一常用】
What's one of your happiest memories?【第二常用】
（你最快樂的回憶是什麼？）
What's the happiest time you remember from your past?
（你記憶中，過去最快樂的時刻是什麼時候？）【第六常用】
【*from the past* 以前】

Tell me the happiest memory you have.【第三常用】
（告訴我你最快樂的回憶。）
Please share a happy memory with me.【第四常用】
（請告訴我一個令你快樂的回憶。）
Please recall a happy memory for me.【第五常用】
（請為我回想一個快樂的回憶。）
【share〔ʃɛr〕*v.* 分享　　recall〔rɪ'kɔl〕*v.* 回想】

## Answers 89

*Every New Year's Eve.*
*I love getting red envelopes.*
*It's an exciting happy holiday.*

□ 答對　□ 答錯

　　*Every New Year's Eve.* 的意思是「每年除夕。」(= *It's every New Year's Eve.*) 也可説成: Every Chinese New Year. (每年的農曆新年。) *I love getting red envelopes.* 的意思是「我喜歡拿紅包。」(= *I love getting money in red envelopes.*) *It's an exciting happy holiday.* 的意思是「那天是一個令人興奮又愉快的假日。」【eve〔iv〕*n.* 前夕　*red envelope* 紅包】

小學生活往往都是快樂的:

　　My elementary school days were special.
　　(我小學時的生活非常特別。)
　　I had wonderful friends and teachers.
　　(我有很棒的朋友和老師。)
　　I was happy almost every day. (我幾乎每天都很快樂。)
　　【*elementary school* 小學】

通過考試,考上學校,往往是最快樂的回憶:

　　It was passing the entrance exam. (就是通過入學考試。)
　　It was getting accepted into a good school.
　　(就是考上好學校。)
　　That was the happiest day for me.
　　(那是我最快樂的一天。)
　　【*entrance exam* 入學考試　accept〔ək'sɛpt〕*v.* 接受】

**Question 90**

# *How often do you rent videos?*

（未回答前，勿翻下一頁）

\* rent〔rɛnt〕*v.* 租　　video〔'vɪdɪo〕*n.* 錄影帶

*How often do you rent videos?* 從前只有錄影帶的時候，意思是「你多久租一次錄影帶？」雖然 video 是指「錄影帶」，但它也包含 VCD 和 DVD，因為 VCD 是 video cassette disk（影音光碟）的縮寫；DVD 是 digital video disk（數位影音光碟）【video〔'vɪdɪ‚o〕*adj.* 電視影像的】所以，現在不管你是去租錄影帶、VCD 或 DVD，都可用 video 這個字。

*How often do you rent videos?* 的意思有三個：①你多久租一次錄影帶？②你多久租一次 VCD？③你多久租一次 DVD？

【比較1】 *How often do you rent videos?*【常用】
　　　　 How often do you rent VCDs?【少用】
　　　　 （你多久租一次 VCD？）
　　　　 How often do you rent DVDs?【少用】
　　　　 （你多久租一次 DVD？）

【比較2】 下面兩句話意思不同：

　　　　 *How often do you rent videos?*
　　　　 （你多久租一次錄影帶、VDC，或 DVD？）
　　　　 Do you rent videos often?
　　　　 （你有沒有常常租錄影帶、VCD 或 DVD？）

## Answers 90

*I rent videos once or twice a month.*
*I love to watch movies.*
*I'm a big movie fan.*

□ 答對　□ 答錯

\* once〔wʌns〕*adv.* 一次　　twice〔twaɪs〕*adv.* 兩次
fan〔fæn〕*n.* 迷

　　*I rent videos once or twice a month.* 的意思是「我每個月租一、兩次錄影帶、VCD 或 DVD。」*I love to watch movies.* 的意思是「我很喜歡看電影。」也可說成：I love to watch movies on DVD.（我喜歡看 DVD 的電影。）*I'm a big movie fan.*（我是超級電影迷。）

如果你有會員卡，你就可以說：

　　I rent videos every week.（我每個禮拜都租 DVD。）
　　I have a video store membership card.
　　（我有 DVD 出租店的會員卡。）
　　I enjoy watching DVDs.（我喜歡看 DVD。）
　　membership〔'mɛmbɚˌʃɪp〕*n.* 會員的資格
　　*membership card* 會員卡

如果你不常租，就可以說：

　　Not very often.（不是很常租。）
　　This year I've been too busy.（今年我太忙了。）
　　I used to rent many last year.（去年我租很多。）
　　【*used to V.* 以前~】

## Questions 81~90　問一答三自我測驗

你光會說，不會寫，可能會漏說 ed 或 s，而你自己不知道，
可是外國人聽起來就不舒服。你一定要經過筆試測驗的練
習，你說出來的話才正確無誤。

81. Question：What's your ideal job?

Answers：_____

_____

_____

82. Question：Who is the person you admire most?

Answers：_____

_____

_____

83. Question：Are you nearsighted?

Answers：_____

_____

_____

84. Question：Do you like to read?

Answers：_____

_____

_____

85. Question：How much TV do you watch?

Answers：_____

_____

_____

86. Question: How do I get to your home?

    Answers: _____

    _____

    _____

87. Question: Where's the nearest ATM?

    Answers: _____

    _____

    _____

88. Question: What's tomorrow's forecast?

    Answers: _____

    _____

    _____

89. Question: What's your happiest memory?

    Answers: _____

    _____

    _____

90. Question: How often do you rent videos?

    Answers: _____

    _____

    _____

※ 你寫完後，須訂正答案，將錯誤的地方，用紅筆標出來，
　 以後說的時候，你就不會漏掉了。

┌─ Question 91 ─┐

# *How much was that?*

（未回答前，勿翻下一頁）

*How much was that?* 的意思是「那個多少錢？」如果問襯衫，就說：How much was that shirt?（那件襯衫多少錢？）如果問鞋子，就說：How much were those shoes?（那雙鞋子多少錢？）如果問手錶，就說：How much was that watch?（那支手錶多少錢？）如果對不熟的朋友，該說：May I ask, "How much was that?"（可不可以請問你：「那個多少錢？」）

下面是美國人常說的話：

**How much was that?**【第一常用】
How much was it?（它要多少錢？）【第二常用】

How much did it cost?（它值多少錢？）【第三常用】
How much did it cost you?【第六常用】
（它花了你多少錢？）
【cost〔kɔst〕v. 值…價錢；使（某人）花費（錢）】

How much did you pay?（你付了多少錢？）【第四常用】
How much did you pay for it?【第七常用】
（你付了多少錢買它？）【pay〔pe〕v. 付錢】

What was the price?（價格是多少？）【第五常用】
What price did you pay for that?【第八常用】
（你買那個東西價格是多少錢？）【price〔praɪs〕n. 價格】

## Answers 91

**_It was three hundred._**

**_It cost three hundred._**

**_I paid around three hundred dollars._**

□答對　□答錯

\* around〔ə'raʊnd〕*adv.* 大約

　　*It was three hundred.* 的意思是「三百塊錢。」也可以只說：Three hundred. ( 三百元。) *It cost three hundred.* ( 它值三百元。) ( = *It cost me three hundred to buy it.* ) *I paid around three hundred dollars.* 的意思是「我大約付了三百塊錢。」( = *I paid about three hundred.* )

如果你不想說價錢，就可說：

　　I can't remember. ( 我不記得了。)

　　I really don't know. ( 我真的不知道。)

　　I got it a long time ago. ( 我很久以前買的。)

　　【get 在此作「買」解】

如果是別人送的，你就可以說：

　　I didn't pay for it. ( 我沒付錢。)

　　It was a gift. ( 它是個禮物。)

　　Someone gave it to me. ( 有人送我的。)

　　【gift〔gɪft〕*n.* 禮物】

# *How are you feeling right now?*

（未回答前，勿翻下一頁）

* ***right now*** 現在

在口試的時候，或美國朋友之間，會常問到：***How are you feeling right now?***（你現在感覺怎樣？）常簡化爲：How are you feeling?（你感覺如何？）使用頻率相同。也可說成：How do you feel right now?（你現在感覺怎樣？）

下面都是美國人常說的話：

> ***How are you feeling right now?***【第一常用】
> How are you feeling at this moment?【第六常用】
> （你現在覺得怎樣？）
> 【moment〔'momənt〕*n.* 時刻】
>
> How do you feel right now?【第二常用】
> （你現在覺得怎樣？）
> How do you feel at this moment?【第七常用】
> （你現在覺得怎樣？）
>
> Are you feeling good today?【第五常用】
> （你今天感覺好嗎？）
> Are you feeling OK?（你覺得還好嗎？）【第四常用】
> Are you feeling all right?【第三常用】
> （你覺得還好吧？）

## Answers 92

> *I feel excited.*
> *I also feel a little nervous.*
> *This is a big day for me.*

□ 答對　□ 答錯

\* excited〔ɪkˋsaɪtɪd〕*adj.* 興奮的
　nervous〔ˋnɝvəs〕*adj.* 緊張的　　big〔bɪg〕*adj.* 重要的

　　這三句話適合口試或和異性朋友約會的時候說。***I feel excited.***
的意思是「我感覺很興奮。」可加強語氣說成：I feel really excited
at this moment.（我現在覺得非常興奮。）雖然句子是現在進行式，
在這裡也可用現在式回答。

　　問：How are you feeling right now?
　　答：***I feel excited.***【較常用】
　　　　I'm feeling excited.【常用】

　　***I also feel a little nervous.*** 的意思是「我也感覺到有點緊張。」
可簡化為：I also feel nervous.（我也感到緊張。）***This is a big day***
***for me.*** 的意思是「今天對我很重要。」( = *This is an important day*
*for me.*)也可說成：Today is important for me.（今天對我很重要。）

也可拍馬屁地說：

　　I feel wonderful.（我覺得很棒。）
　　I'm very happy to be here.（能來這裡我覺得很高興。）
　　It's a pleasure to be speaking with you.
　　（和你談話是我的榮幸。）【pleasure〔ˋplɛʒɚ〕*n.* 樂趣；榮幸】

**Question 93**

# *How tall are you?*

（未回答前，勿翻下一頁）

　　***How tall are you?*** 的意思是「你多高？」不能説成：*How high are you?*（誤）可加長爲：I'd like to know, "How tall are you?"（我想要知道：「你多高？」）或 I'm curious as to how tall you are.（我很想知道你有多高。）

【curious〔ˈkjʊrɪəs〕*adj.* 好奇的；想知道的　*as to* 至於；關於】

下面是美國人常説的話，我們按照使用頻率排列：

① ***How tall are you?***【第一常用】

② What's your height?【第二常用】
　　（你有多高？）【height〔haɪt〕*n.* 身高】

③ What is your height?【第三常用】
　　（你有多高？）

④ How many centimeters tall are you?
　　（你身高幾公分？）

⑤ May I ask your height?
　　（我可以問你有多高嗎？）

【centimeter〔ˈsɛntəˌmitɚ〕*n.* 公分】

*How tall are you?*

## Answers 93

*I'm not very tall.*

*Everyone in my family is short.*

*I'm 155 centimeters tall.*

□答對　□答錯

*I'm not very tall.* 的意思是「我不是很高。」*Everyone in my family is short.* 的意思是「我家裡的每一個人都矮。」【short〔ʃɔrt〕*adj.* 矮的】*I'm 155 centimeters tall.*（我身高 155 公分。）【155 要唸成：one hundred and fifty-five】在全世界，除美國以 foot（英尺）、inch（英寸）量身高外，其他都用 centimeter（公分）。

如果你不高也不矮，就可以說：

　　I'm not considered tall.（我不被認為高。）

　　I'm not considered short.（我不被認為矮。）

　　I'm of average height.（我屬於一般高度。）

　　【consider〔kən'sɪdə〕*v.* 認為　average〔'ævərɪdʒ〕*adj.* 一般的】

如果你很高，就可以說：

　　I'm almost 170 centimeters.（我將近 170 公分。）

　　I'm pretty tall for my age.

　　（對我這個年紀而言，我是相當高的。）

　　I'm taller than most of my friends.

　　（我比我大多數的朋友都要高。）

　　【pretty〔'prɪtɪ〕*adv.* 相當；非常地】

Question 94

# *What's something you're really good at?*

（未回答前，勿翻下一頁）

*What's something you're really good at?* 的意思是「你擅長什麼？」可以加強語氣說成：What's something you're really good at doing? ( 你擅長做什麼？ ) really 有「真地；很；非常」的意思，在此作「非常」解。

【*be good at* 擅長；精通】

下面是美國人常說的話：

*What's something you're really good at?* 【第一常用】
What are you good at? 【第二常用】
( 你擅長什麼？ )
What are you good at doing? 【第三常用】
( 你擅長做什麼？ )

What are you able to do very well? 【第六常用】
( 你能夠做什麼做得非常好？ )
What can you do very well? 【第四常用】
( 你能把什麼做得非常好？ )
What are you talented at doing? 【第五常用】
( 你擅長做什麼？ )

【*be able to V.* 能夠～　talented〔ˈtæləntɪd〕*adj.* 有才能的】

## Answers 94

*I'm good at speaking English.*
*I like learning English a lot.*
*My English scores are always high.*

□ 答對　□ 答錯

\* score〔skor〕 *n.* 分數

*I'm good at speaking English.* 的意思是「我擅長說英文。」可以加強語氣說成：I'm pretty good at speaking English.（我很擅長說英文。）可簡化爲：I'm good at English.（我精通英文。）*I like learning English a lot.* 的意思是「我很喜歡學英文。」(=*I like to learn English a lot.*) 〔a lot = very much〕*My English scores are always high.* 的意思是「我的英文分數總是很高。」(=*My English scores are always good.*)

如果你喜歡唱歌，可說：

I love to sing.（我喜歡唱歌。）
Everyone says I have good voice.
　　（大家都說我的聲音很好。）〔voice〔vɔɪs〕*n.* 聲音〕
I often go to KTVs.（我常去 KTV。）

如果你善於交朋友，就可以說：

I'm good at making friends.（我擅長交朋友。）
I have many friends.（我有很多朋友。）
I am popular in my class.（我在班上很受歡迎。）
　　【*make friends* 交朋友　　popular〔'pɑpjələ〕*adj.* 受歡迎的】

Question 95

# *Tell me about your home.*

（未回答前，勿翻下一頁）

*Tell me about your home.* 的意思是「告訴我有關你家
的情形。」也可說成：Tell me about your place. ( 告訴我
有關你家的情形。)【place〔ples〕*n.* 住所；地方】或 Tell me
about the place where you live. ( 告訴我有關你所住的地
方。)

下面是美國人常說的話，我們按照使用頻率排列：

① *Tell me about your home.*【第一常用】

② Describe your home.【第二常用】
（描述一下你的家。）

③ Describe the place where you live.【第三常用】
（描述一下你住的地方。）
【describe〔dɪ'skraɪb〕*v.* 描述；形容】

④ What's your home like?
（你的家是什麼樣子？）

⑤ What's the place where you live like?
（你住的地方是什麼樣子？）

⑥ How many bedrooms does your home have?
（你家有幾間臥房？）
【bedroom〔'bɛd,rum〕*n.* 臥房】

**Answers 95**

*My home is in the city.*
*I live in a high-rise building.*
*My apartment has three bedrooms.*

□ 答對　□ 答錯

* high-rise〔ˈhaɪˈraɪz〕*adj.* 高層的；多層的
  ***high-rise building*** 高層建築物（= *many-storeyed building* ）
  apartment〔əˈpɑrtmənt〕*n.* 公寓

　　***My home is in the city.*** 的意思是「我的家在城市。」(= *I
live in the city.* ) ***I live in a high-rise building.*** 的意思是「我
住在高樓裡。」***My apartment has three bedrooms.*** 的意思是
「我的公寓有三間臥房。」

如果你和父母住，你就可以說：

　　I live with my parents.（我和父母住。）
　　Our home is traditional.（我家是傳統的；我家是老式的。）
　　It's comfortable and clean.（它非常舒適而且乾淨。）
　　traditional〔trəˈdɪʃənḷ〕*adj.* 傳統的
　　comfortable〔ˈkʌmfətəbḷ〕*adj.* 舒適的

如果你自己在外面租房子，你就可以說：

　　My place is a small apartment.（我家是間小公寓。）
　　It's near my school.（靠近我的學校。）
　　I share it with two friends.（我和兩個朋友一起住。）
　　【share〔ʃɛr〕*v.* 分享；共用】

Question 96

# *Do you enjoy shopping?*

（未回答前，勿翻下一頁）

\* enjoy〔ɪn'dʒɔɪ〕 *v.* 喜歡　shop〔ʃɑp〕 *v.* 購物

*Do you enjoy shopping?* 的意思是「你喜不喜歡買東西？」源自：Do you enjoy going shopping? ( 你喜不喜歡去買東西。) 如果只是喜歡逛街不買東西，就要說成：Do you enjoy window-shopping? ( 你喜不喜歡逛街瀏覽櫥窗？)
【window-shopping〔'wɪndo'ʃɑpɪŋ〕 *n.* 瀏覽櫥窗】

下面是美國人常說的話，我們按照使用頻率排列：

① *Do you enjoy shopping?* 【第一常用】
② Do you like to shop? 【第二常用】
　　( 你喜歡買東西嗎？)
③ Do you shop a lot? 【第三常用】
　　( 你常常買東西嗎？) 【*a lot* 常常】

④ Are you crazy about shopping?
　　( 你熱愛買東西嗎？)
⑤ Are you a big shopper? ( 你很愛買東西嗎？)
⑥ Are you someone who loves to shop?
　　( 你是個愛買東西的人嗎？)

　　crazy〔'krezɪ〕 *adj.* 瘋狂的；很喜歡的
　　shopper〔'ʃɑpɚ〕 *n.* 購物者

## Answers 96

*Yes, I do.*

*I love to go shopping.*

*It's relaxing and fun.*

□ 答對　□ 答錯

---

\* relaxing〔rɪ'læksɪŋ〕*adj.* 令人放鬆的

　fun〔fʌn〕*adj.* 好玩的；有趣的

*Yes, I do.* 在這裡的意思是「是的，我喜歡。」(=*Yes, I enjoy shopping.*) 可加強語氣說成：Yes, I do very much. (是的，我非常喜歡。) *I love to go shopping.* 的意思是「我愛買東西。」*It's relaxing and fun.* 的意思是「它輕鬆又有趣。」可加強語氣說成：It's both relaxing and fun. (它既輕鬆又有趣。)

也可這樣回答：

　Of course, I do. (當然，我喜歡。)

　Shopping is interesting. (買東西很有趣。)

　It's fun to look for bargains. (去找便宜的東西很好玩。)

　【bargain〔'bɑrgɪn〕*n.* 便宜貨】

如果不喜歡買東西，就可以說：

　I hate to go shopping. (我不喜歡去逛街買東西。)

　It's like torture to me. (那對我來說，像是種折磨。)

　I let others buy things for me. (我會讓別人幫我買東西。)

　【hate〔het〕*v.* 討厭；不喜歡　torture〔'tɔrtʃɚ〕*n.* 折磨】

Question 97

# *Have you ever given a speech?*

（未回答前，勿翻下一頁）

* ever〔'ɛvɚ〕*adv.* 曾經　　speech〔spitʃ〕*n.* 演講
*give a speech* 發表演說

***Have you ever given a speech?*** 的意思是「你有沒有曾經演講過？」可以加長為：Have you ever given a speech before?（你以前有沒有演講過？）或 Have you ever given a speech in front of many people before?（你以前有沒有在很多人面前演講過？）【*in front of* 在…面前】美國人也常簡化為：Ever given a speech before?（以前演講過嗎？）

「演講；發表演說」的說法很多，歸納如下：

**give a speech**【第一常用】
= deliver a speech【第三常用】
= make a speech【第二常用】

= give a lecture【第六常用】
= deliver a lecture【第七常用】

= give an address【第五常用】
= deliver an address【第四常用】

【deliver〔dɪ'lɪvɚ〕*v.* 發表（演講）　　lecture〔'lɛktʃɚ〕*n.* 演講】

在字典上，address 有兩個發音：①〔ə'drɛs〕②〔'ædrɛs〕，但是美國人唸〔ə'drɛs〕時，常表示「演講」；唸〔'ædrɛs〕時，通常表示「住址」。

## Answers 97

*I did once.*

*I gave a speech in class.*

*I was extremely nervous.*

□ 答對　　□ 答錯

---

\* once〔wʌns〕*adv.* 一次　　extremely〔ɪk'strimlɪ〕*adv.* 非常
nervous〔'nɝvəs〕*adj.* 緊張的

*I did once.* 的意思是「我演講過一次。」( = *I gave a speech
once.* ) *I gave a speech in class.* ( 我在班上演講過。) ( = *I
gave a speech in my class.* ) *I was extremely nervous.* 的
意思是「我非常緊張。」

如果你做過幾次演講，你就可以說：

I have given several speeches. ( 我做過幾次演講。)
I study English by giving speeches.
( 我藉由發表演說學英文。)
It's the best way to learn. ( 這是最好的學習方式。)

如果你從未演講過，就可以說：

No, I never have. ( 不，我從來沒有過。)
I'm afraid of public speaking. ( 我害怕公開演說。)
I am too nervous and shy. ( 我太緊張、太害羞了。)
*be afraid of* 害怕　　public〔'pʌblɪk〕*adj.* 公開的
shy〔ʃaɪ〕*adj.* 害羞的

## Question 98

# *Would you rather be single or married?*

（未回答前，勿翻下一頁）

* *would rather* 寧願
single〔'sɪŋḷ〕*adj.* 單身的　　married〔'mærɪd〕*adj.* 已婚的

　　*Would you rather be single or married?* 的意思是「你寧願單身還是結婚？」可以加長為：If you could choose, would you rather be single or be married?（如果你可以選擇，你寧願單身還是結婚？）be married 也可說成 get married。

下面是美國人常說的話：

*Would you rather be single or married?*【第一常用】
Would you like to get married someday?【第三常用】
（將來有一天，你會想要結婚嗎？）
【someday〔'sʌm,de〕*adv.* 將來有一天】

Do you want to remain single all your life?【第四常用】
（你想一輩子保持單身嗎？）
Do you ever want to marry?（你曾經想要結婚嗎？）【第二常用】
remain〔rɪ'men〕*v.* 保持　　ever〔'ɛvɚ〕*adv.* 曾經
marry〔'mærɪ〕*v.* 結婚

What's your opinion on being single or being married?
（你對單身或結婚的看法如何？）【第五常用】
What are your views on remaining single or being
　　married?（你對保持單身或結婚的看法如何？）【第六常用】
【opinion〔ə'pɪnjən〕*n.* 意見；看法　　view〔vju〕*n.* 看法】

## Answers 98

*I'd rather be single.*
*I like to be free.*
*I'm an independent person.*

□ 答對　□ 答錯

* independent〔͵ɪndɪˈpɛndənt〕*adj.* 獨立的；獨立性強的

*I'd rather be single.* 的意思是「我寧願單身。」( = *I prefer being single.* ) *I like to be free.* 的意思是「我喜歡自由。」( = *I like being free.* ) *I'm an independent person.* 的意思是「我很獨立。」( = *I'm independent.* )

如果你想結婚，就可說：

I'd like to get married. ( 我想要結婚。)
I want to have a family. ( 我想要有個家庭。)
Having kids seems like fun. ( 有小孩似乎很有趣。)
【seem〔sim〕*v.* 似乎　　fun〔fʌn〕*n.* 有趣的事】

如果你不知道，就可回答：

That's a good question. ( 那是個好問題。)
I don't know the answer. ( 我不知道答案。)
Either way is OK with me. ( 我覺得結不結婚都可以。)
either〔ˈiðɚ〕*pron.* ( 兩者 ) 任一
way〔we〕*n.* 方式；樣子

# *How do you celebrate Chinese New Year?*

（未回答前，勿翻下一頁）

美國人喜歡問中國人：*How do you celebrate Chinese New Year?* (你們怎麼慶祝中國新年？) 中國人所說的「農曆新年」(Lunar New Year)，外國人並不知道。

下面都是美國人可能問的問題：

*How do you celebrate Chinese New Year?*【第一常用】
How do you enjoy Chinese New Year?【第三常用】
( 你們如何過中國新年？)

What do you do on Chinese New Year?【第二常用】
( 你們在中國新年會做什麼？)
What special things do you do during Chinese New
　　Year? ( 在中國新年期間，你們會做什麼特別的事？)【第五常用】
What customs do you follow on Chinese New Year?
( 在農曆新年，你們會遵循什麼習俗？)【第四常用】
【custom (ˈkʌstəm) n. 習俗　　follow (ˈfɑlo) v. 遵循】

Do you have a party on Chinese New Year?【第六常用】
( 你們在中國新年會舉行聚會嗎？)
Do you have a special celebration for Chinese New
　　Year? ( 你們在中國新年會有特別的慶祝活動嗎？)【第七常用】
【celebration (ˌsɛləˈbreʃən) n. 慶祝活動】

## Answers 99

*My family is very traditional.*

*We follow all the Chinese customs.*

*We have a party, a feast, and lots of visitors.*

□答對　□答錯

---

\* traditional〔trə'dɪʃənḷ〕 *adj.* 傳統的
feast〔fist〕 *n.* 盛宴　　visitor〔'vɪzɪtɚ〕 *n.* 訪客

*My family is very traditional.* 的意思是「我們家非常傳統。」*We follow all the Chinese customs.* 的意思是「我們遵循所有中國的風俗。」*We have a party, a feast, and lots of visitors.* 的意思是「我們有聚會、吃大餐,和很多客人。」(= *We have a party, a big dinner, and lots of guests.*)

如果你會和家人出國渡假,就可說:

My family travels overseas. ( 我們全家人會出國旅遊。)
We love to visit new places. ( 我們喜歡到新的地方玩。)
New Year is the best time to get away.
( 新年是出門最好的時間。)

overseas〔'ovɚ'siz〕 *adv.* 到國外
*get away* 離開;出門 (= *go to some places*)

也可以幽默地說:

I just relax and eat. ( 我就只是放鬆和吃東西。)
I watch a lot of TV. ( 我看很多電視。)
I also visit many friends. ( 我也拜訪很多朋友。)

Question 100

# *How much sleep do you need?*

（未回答前，勿翻下一頁）

*How much sleep do you need?* 的意思是「你需要多少睡眠？」可加長為：How much sleep do you need every night? （你每天晚上需要多少睡眠？）every night 也可説成 each night。

下面是美國人常説的話，我們按照使用頻率排列：

① *How much sleep do you need?*【第一常用】

② How many hours of sleep do you need?【第二常用】
（你需要幾個小時的睡眠？）

③ What's a good night's sleep for you?【第三常用】
（對你來說，什麼才算晚上睡了個好覺？）

④ For a good night's rest, how many hours do you
need? （晚上想好好休息，你需要幾個小時的睡眠？）

⑤ To do a good job, how many hours of sleep do
you need? （想要好好工作，你需要幾個小時的睡眠？）
【rest〔rɛst〕*n.* 休息】

⑥ What's the minimum amount of sleep time that
you need? （你最少需要幾個小時的睡眠時間？）

⑦ What are the ideal number of hours for a restful sleep?
（要好好休息睡覺的話，最理想的睡眠時間是幾個小時？）
minimum〔'mɪnəməm〕*adj.* 最小的
ideal〔aɪ'diəl〕*adj.* 理想的　　number〔'nʌmbɚ〕*n.* 數目
restful〔'rɛstfəl〕*adj.* 休息充足的

### Answers 100

*I need at least seven.*

*I prefer eight or nine.*

*Less than seven, and I'll still feel tired.*

□ 答對　□ 答錯

---

\* *at least* 至少　　prefer〔prɪˈfɝ〕*v.* 比較喜歡

*I need at least seven.* 的意思是「我至少需要七個小時。」
( = *I need at least seven hours.* ) *I prefer eight or nine.* 的意思是「我比較喜歡八或九個小時。」*Less than seven, and I'll still feel tired.* 的意思是「少於七個小時，我仍然會感到疲倦。」( = *If I sleep less than seven hours, I'll still feel tired.* )

如果你睡得少，就可說：

I'm lucky. ( 我很幸運。)
I only need five or six hours. ( 我只需要五或六個小時。)
But I always take a nap after lunch.
( 但我吃完午餐後，總是會睡個午覺。)
【nap〔næp〕*n.* 小睡　*take a nap* 小睡片刻】

如果你喜歡睡覺，你就可說：

I need about ten. ( 我需要大約十小時。)
I love to sleep. ( 我很喜歡睡覺。)
Regrettably, I only get about seven hours.
( 令人遺憾的是，我只睡大約七個小時。)
【regrettably〔rɪˈgrɛtəblɪ〕*adv.* 可惜；令人遺憾地】

## Questions 91~100　問一答三自我測驗

你已經背到最後一回了，不要忘記寫完這回測驗後，要複習前面，默寫錯誤的地方。

91. Question : How much was that?

    Answers : _____

    _____

    _____


92. Question : How are you feeling right now?

    Answers : _____

    _____

    _____


93. Question : How tall are you?

    Answers : _____

    _____

    _____


94. Question : What's something you're really good at?

    Answers : _____

    _____

    _____


95. Question : Tell me about your home.

    Answers : _____

    _____

    _____

96. Question: Do you enjoy shopping?

    Answers: _____

              _____

              _____

97. Question: Have you ever given a speech?

    Answers: _____

              _____

              _____

98. Question: Would you rather be single or married?

    Answers: _____

              _____

              _____

99. Question: How do you celebrate Chinese New Year?

    Answers: _____

              _____

              _____

100. Question: How much sleep do you need?

    Answers: _____

              _____

              _____

※ 恭喜你寫完了！要不斷地聽 CD 複習。

# 📄 問一答三英語 索引

Are you nearsighted? 181

Are you OK? 97

Can you cook? 169

Can you lend me 100 dollars? 25

Can you play any instruments? 125

Can you swim? 119

Did you sleep well? 117

Do you belong to any clubs? 161

Do you enjoy shopping? 209

Do you have a nickname? 171

Do you have any pets? 141

Do you like learning English? 127

Do you like to read? 183

Good-bye. 93

Good morning. 39

Have you ever been abroad? 55

Have you ever given a speech? 211

Have you ever gone camping? 151

Here or to go? 149

How are you? 5

How are you feeling right now? 201

How did you get here today? 135

How do I get to your home? 187

How do you celebrate Chinese New Year? 215

How do you celebrate your birthday? 173

How do you do? 19

How do you go to school? 49

How do you like this weather? 85

How long will you be gone? 107

How many are in your class? 123

How many are in your family? 11

How many languages can you speak? 121

How much sleep do you need? 217

How much TV do you watch? 185

How much was that? 199

How often do you exercise? 89

How often do you rent videos? 195

How old are you? 3

How tall are you? 203

How was the test? 29

I like your shirt. 95

I'm sorry. 91

Make yourself at home. 23

May I ask what you do? 71

May I ask you a question? 113

May I ask your name? 1

Mind if I join you? 103

Need any help? 27

Tell me about your home. 207

Tell me about yourself. 159

Thank you. 69

Want to grab a bite? 77

What are you doing this weekend? 13

What are you doing tonight? 133

What are your future plans? 35

What are your hobbies? 9

What are your summer plans? 99

What day is today? 47

What did you do yesterday? 59

What did you eat for breakfast? 31

What did you eat last night? 129

What do you do when you get sick? 163

What do you usually eat for lunch? 139

What do you want to do? 111

What do your parents do? 63

What grade are you in? 33

What kind of movies do you like? 61

What's new? 105

What's something you hate to do? 147

What's something you're really good at? 205

What's the date today? 53

What's tomorrow's forecast? 191

What's your favorite food? 41

What's your favorite fruit? 115

What's your favorite season? 145

What's your favorite sport? 101

What's your favorite subject? 67

What's your happiest memory? 193

What's your ideal job? 177

What's your phone number? 57

What time do you get up? 167

What time do you go to bed? 37

What time is it? 17

What type of music do you like? 143

What would you like to drink? 75

When are you free? 79

When is your birthday? 51

When you feel depressed, what do you do? 155

Where are you from? 83

Where are you going? 73

Where did you get that shirt? 157

Where do you live? 7

Where's the bathroom? 45

Where's the nearest ATM? 189

Where's your favorite place to go? 81

Which country would you like to visit? 165

Who is the person you admire most? 179

Who is your best friend? 137

Who is your favorite teacher? 15

Would you rather be single or married? 213